Mia

T0347244

THROUGH MY EYES
AUSTRALIAN DISASTER ZONES

Tyenna (Tasmania)

Mia (Western Australia)

Alex (South Australia)

THROUGH MY EYES
NATURAL DISASTER ZONES

Hotaka (Japan)

Shaozhen (China)

Lyla (New Zealand)

Angel (Philippines)

THROUGH MY EYES

Shahana (Kashmir)

Amina (Somalia)

Naveed (Afghanistan)

Emilio (Mexico)

Malini (Sri Lanka)

Zafir (Syria)

Hasina (Myanmar)

THROUGH MY EYES AUSTRALIAN DISASTER ZONES

series editor Lyn White

DIANNE WOLFER

ALLEN&UNWIN
SYDNEY · MELBOURNE · AUCKLAND · LONDON

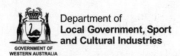

Department of
**Local Government, Sport
and Cultural Industries**
GOVERNMENT OF
WESTERN AUSTRALIA

First published by Allen & Unwin in 2022

Allen & Unwin
Cammeraygal Country
83 Alexander Street
Crows Nest NSW 2065
Australia
Phone: (61 2) 8425 0100
Email: info@allenandunwin.com
Web: www.allenandunwin.com

*Allen & Unwin acknowledges the Traditional Owners of the Country on which we
live and work. We pay our respects to all Aboriginal and Torres Strait Islander
Elders, past and present.*

A catalogue record for this
book is available from the
National Library of Australia

ISBN 978 1 76087 702 6

For teaching resources, explore www.allenandunwin.com/resources/for-teachers

Cover and text design by Sandra Nobes
Cover photos: girl – Can Stock/Armin Staudt; sky – Shutterstock/Naeblys;
landscape – Shutterstock/anne-tipodees
Map design by Guy Holt
Set in 11/15 pt Plantin by Midland Typesetters, Australia
This book was printed in June 2022 by McPherson's Printing Group, Australia.

10 9 8 7 6 5 4 3 2 1

This story takes place in the Pilbara region of Western Australia, on the lands of the Ngarluma, Yindjibarndi and Banyjima people. We acknowledge the traditional owners of these lands, who belong to the oldest continuing culture in the world and who have cared for and protected Country for thousands of years. We honour them and pay our respects to their elders, past, present and emerging.

The novel is set during Cyclone Veronica which occurred in the Pilbara in 2019. The characters and some of the locations are fictional, to protect the privacy of communities and individuals. We have also altered some details and the chronology of various events, for the sake of the story, but the essential truths of the devastation caused by the cyclone remain.

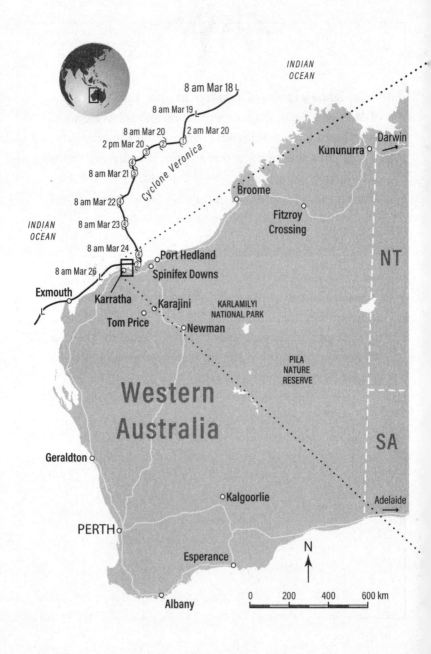

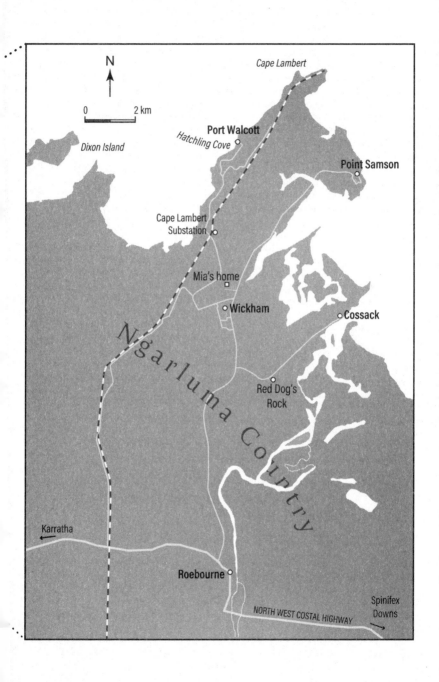

One

||||||||||||||||||||||||||||||||||||||||||||||||||||||||||||||||||||||||||||||||||

Netting cuts into Mia's flesh. She can't breathe. Her arms flail as she struggles to keep her head above water. Wild screeching echoes over black waves as the weight of the net drags her deeper. Mia gasps, but instead of saltwater, she gulps muggy Pilbara air.

She opens her eyes, sweat soaking her back. The nightmare felt so real. Mia hears the screeching again.

'Okay, I'm awake,' she calls to the corellas outside her window.

Their squawking starts around six every morning. The birds are more reliable than any alarm clock. That's good on school days, but not so fun on weekends when she wants to sleep in.

Mia takes three deep breaths, gazing around her room as her heart rate settles. The fan is gently turning, posters of horses and turtles cover the walls, and books are piled everywhere. She opens her curtain, banishing the frightening underwater images.

Since her first nightmare last year, Mia's learned

coping strategies with the help of the school counsellor. Now, most of her dreams are peaceful, but remembering that first nightmare still rattles her.

Mia was in the ocean, flailing through a maze of sea plastic and tangled sea creatures. The bed felt like it was dissolving. The nightmare replayed for weeks. Mia woke every night, her mind filled with images of dolphins caught in ghost nets, and seabirds choking on plastic. Then there was the other dream about flooded turtle nests . . .

She looks out the window. The vast Pilbara sky is cloudy and grey, but there's no rain falling. That means Mum's equine therapy classes can go ahead.

The wet season won't finish for another six weeks, but today Mum is restarting riding sessions. Her regulars said they were desperate for some horse-time. So far, it's been a quiet wet season. Around five cyclones usually develop in the warm waters off Western Australia during the wet, but so far the only cyclone to threaten the Pilbara this year has been Riley. That one stayed well offshore.

Mia watches the heavy clouds jostle. 'Don't rain before midday,' she tells them.

A fly buzzes along the windowsill. As Mia opens the latch to shoo it out, she feels a blast of heat. Across the yard, she can see the horses flicking their tails and tossing their manes. She sprays eucalyptus aerosol on her face. Flies hate the smell.

Mia pulls on her jodhpurs and rummages through her messy wardrobe. Where's her horseriding shirt?

Maybe Mum washed it. Mia runs along the hallway in her bra, opens the back door and dashes out to the washing line. There it is, flapping in the breeze. She shrugs on the cotton shirt. It clings to her skin in the humid air.

She stops for a moment to gaze around their property. Pilbara Animal Care is a twelve-hectare block, down a dirt track, off the road connecting Roebourne and Point Samson. For Mia, it's the best thing in the world being tucked away in the bush with so much open space, five kilometres from Wickham, a small town in the middle of nowhere.

She buttons her shirt and walks down the hallway to join her mother in the kitchen. Mum's ready for equine therapy classes in riding pants and an indigo shirt with the vet logo Mia designed for her. It's a horse surrounded by mulla-mulla, her mother's favourite flower.

'Morning – thanks for washing my shirt.'

Mum smiles. 'How did you sleep?' Her voice is casual, but her worried brown eyes give her away.

'Mm, fine . . .' Nightmares are the last thing Mia wants to talk about today.

'Great.' Mum kisses her forehead, then pushes back her long dark hair. 'Toast, porridge or muesli?'

'Toast, please.'

While Mum sips tea and checks their morning schedule, Mia spreads their neighbour Jimmy's mango jam across her toast.

'How many are coming today?' she asks between mouthfuls.

'Six regulars and two new riders.'

'Rosa?'

'Of course! She's your first one.'

Mia grins. Rosa is a bouncy, totally horse-mad seven-year-old who's been coming to Saturday sessions for two years. She's Deaf, and last year Mia mastered enough Auslan to have short conversations with her. She licks jam off her fingers and practises signing a few instructions: *stop, go, loosen the reins.*

'I'm heading over to the office.' Mum grabs her hat from a hook on the wall before stepping onto the wide front veranda. 'See you there.'

'Okay, won't be long.' Mia swallows her last bite. 'I'll just brush my teeth.'

She heads down the hallway to the bathroom, flicks on the light and steps around a possum in a cage. As well as being a vet and equine therapist, Mum also cares for injured wildlife. Sadly, there's plenty of need for her skills. In the Pilbara, native birds and animals are often hit by cars and the huge road trains taking mining equipment and essentials to remote camps and communities.

'Good morning, Possum,' Mia says. 'Don't worry, I'll be gone in a moment.'

The possum blinks its sleepy eyes.

Mia drags her sun-bleached hair into a ponytail. She glances in the mirror. Her eyes still look a little startled from the nightmare. Mia remembers Dad describing them as two big green olives. She smiles at the memory. It will be good to see him and her other family in the school holidays.

She pulls on her elastic-sided boots and races across the yard. Their stable is by the gate, next to Mum's office and surgery.

As Mia opens the gate their horses crowd around her. She gives them each a hug, then tickles Bandit's soft muzzle, inhaling his warm, horsey smell. Bandit is their cheekiest pony, but she loves him best.

Bandit's stable buddies are Freckles, a miniature pony, and Sultan, a bay-coloured ex-racehorse that Mum rescued last year. Mia fills their feed boxes and gives them a quick brush. She never tires of the way the steady rhythm of horse brushing calms her. Their clients love grooming the animals too. It's a bonding part of their horse-time.

An excited buzz grows in the air as people start to arrive. Mum's riders are mostly children, but locals of all ages come to watch, or just to be around the horses. Some even drive from Karratha, over fifty kilometres away.

Mia watches the little kids milling around Freckles, knowing first-hand how soothing horse-time can be. Being with Bandit helps settle her own anxiety. She thinks back to that first panic attack last year.

They were at Hatchling Cove, ten minutes' drive from home. Mum was repairing a storm-damaged dune and Mia had wandered along the high-tide line, gathering sea-glass to make into jewellery. At the far end of the cove, she stumbled across a dugong. It was tangled in netting.

'Mum,' she yelled. 'Help!' But the wind blew away her words.

The beached dugong gave a weak chirp as Mia's trembling hands tried to loosen the net.

'*Mum!*' she screamed as loud as she could, jumping up and waving her arms.

In the distance, her mother shaded her eyes, staring up the beach. Then she dropped her spade and began running.

Mia scooped water into her hat and poured it over the animal's raw skin. The dugong shuddered.

'Hold on,' she whispered. 'Please don't die.'

Mum arrived at last.

They worked together, loosening and untangling the netting until the beautiful creature was free. But it was far too heavy to drag to safety. Mum phoned the ranger, then they soaked their shirts and squeezed water over its back. The dugong stared into Mia's eyes and something passed between them. It was a moment that words could never explain.

Mia knew the animal was going to die and that there was nothing she could do. She felt utterly helpless as the dugong took its final breath, still gazing into Mia's eyes.

She'd seen death at Mum's surgery, but not like this. Mia's world seemed suddenly less secure. Her heart raced. A choking sensation gripped her chest. Mia gasped for air. For a moment she thought *she* was going to die.

After that her nightmares began. Then, news articles about marine pollution became a magnet for her attention. Mia watched climate change clips compulsively and started gathering fishing boat flotsam from local beaches. There were so many lures, lines and litter. How had she never noticed all this junk before?

Being with animals was the one thing that calmed her. Having lots of horse-time still does. When the counsellor explained that anxiety and panic attacks are not unusual, Mia was relieved and felt less alone.

Since then, she's learned ways to manage symptoms before they take hold. Mia's determined not to let her fears get in the way of becoming a vet like Mum, and following her passion to help endangered wildlife.

'Mia.' Mum waves from across the home yard. 'It's almost time for the first session. Could you bring Bandit over, please?'

'Coming.' Mia pushes away thoughts of stricken wildlife and takes five deep breaths.

Bandit shakes his mane, stepping briskly as Mia leads him towards Mum. Then she goes back to saddle the other horses.

The gate clangs. Mia glances up from buckling Sultan's girth strap. It's Rosa, arriving with a jaunty swagger, wearing her battered Akubra hat and new cowboy boots.

'Hi, Miiia,' Rosa yells in what her family call her Deaf voice. She points to her shiny boots, grins, then drops her bag and runs to the mounting tower.

Rosa swaps the Akubra for a hard hat, then jiggles about as Mia leads the ex-racehorse towards the tower. Sultan whiffles. He loves Rosa as much as she loves him.

When Rosa began riding, they paired her with Freckles, the miniature pony, but once Rosa heard how Mum rescued Sultan from starvation after he'd been dumped in the bush, she begged to be allowed to ride the big bay. Now the two are inseparable. Each week, Sultan greets her with a whiffle or a whinny. Rosa has learned to read every toss of his head.

'Hello, Sultan,' she says with a huge smile.

The racehorse nudges his little rider.

Rosa launches herself into the saddle and takes the reins. She trots around the riding circle with the bravado of a bronco rider, then urges Sultan into a canter. After a few loops he settles back to a trot. Rosa shifts effort-lessly to a graceful rise. Mia laughs with delight. The kid's a natural.

Rosa reins in Sultan, stops, and turns to Mia. 'Let's go,' she signs.

After swinging into Bandit's saddle Mia rides ahead as they leave the home yard and set out on the medium riding circuit. Last October, before the wet season, the horses startled a massive bungarra halfway around. Mia wonders whether they'll see the old lizard today. Sultan barely blinked when the goanna ran in front of them, but Bandit shied, and Mia came a cropper on the red Pilbara dust.

Mia turns in the saddle to make sure everything is

all right. Rosa gives her a thumbs up. Even with a cloudy sky, the bling on her new boots is dazzling.

'Loookk,' Rosa shouts.

Sure enough, the prehistoric-looking lizard is strutting across the scrub, its forked tongue flicking. *Better a bungarra than a snake*, Mia thinks. There are plenty of venomous ones in the Pilbara, and Mia keeps a pressure bandage in her saddlebag just in case. Like most wildlife, she knows that if you don't bother snakes, they're unlikely to bother you.

They wait for the goanna to pass. Rosa balances the reins in one hand and makes a sign with the other hand that Mia doesn't know – palm facing downwards, all fingers in a claw. Rosa moves her hand forward, a bit like a spider. She notices Mia's puzzled expression, so she signs each letter to spell *creepy*.

Mia holds Bandit's reins firm until the bungarra bolts. Then she hooks them over the front of the saddle and reply-signs, 'I like them.' She thinks for a moment, then has a stab at signing, 'Did you see the lovely spots on its baggy skin?'

Rosa giggles and makes a face. Then she signs, 'Lizard,' and something else with an open hand and five fingers against her head, which might be a swear word.

Mia points to her watch. 'Sorry, Rosa, we have to head back soon.'

Rosa frowns, but taps Sultan's belly with her heels. At the end of her half-hour, Rosa usually tries to sneak in extra time. They trot to the tower, where Rosa dismounts and leads Sultan into the stable for a rub-down.

9

More onlookers have arrived while they've been gone. Two children are patting Freckles. She's tossing her mane, loving the attention.

Mia walks Bandit towards their neighbour, who lives in a shack at the end of their lane. Jimmy is a lanky old stockman who can't ride anymore because of his dodgy hips, but being with the horses makes him happy. Others come and go, but since Jimmy's wife died, he's rarely missed a Saturday to come over and sit with the horses.

Jimmy's wise eyes are as blue as dragonfly wings, a startling contrast to the leathery skin of his face. He's like a grandad to Mia and his bitzer dog, Dog, is best buddies with her kelpie, Biff. The two Pilbara dogs have a similar muzzle, so they're probably related.

'Ready for a brew, Dimples?' Jimmy holds up a billy, using his favourite nickname for Mia.

'I'm ready for your damper!'

Jimmy tilts his weathered Akubra hat as she tethers Bandit in the shade.

Each Saturday Jimmy brings home-baked bread wrapped in a tea towel. Between sessions, he spreads his mango jam on the damper and brews tea for everyone in a billy over the campfire, adding a gumleaf or two to flavour the tea.

'It's bonzer watching the riders again,' Jimmy says as he swings the billy in a circle. 'I'm glad your mum didn't wait till the end of the wet season to restart her sessions.'

'Me too,' Mia agrees, between sips of Jimmy's smoky-tasting tea.

She checks her watch. The next rider should be

here any minute. All Mum said was that her name is Erin, and that she'd be riding Bandit.

Right on time, a dust cloud rises over the track and a flash new Land Rover pulls up at their gate. A tall teenager steps out.

Two

||||||||||||||||||||||||||||||||||||||||||||||||||||||||||||||||||||||||||

Mia watches the new girl struggling to unlatch their gate. It's the standard bush-block loop of wire over a hook, so it shouldn't be that hard . . .

The girl manages it at last. As the Land Rover drives through, Jimmy nods to the L-plates.

'Fancy wheels for a newbie,' he chuckles, scratching his bristly chin.

Mum chats briefly with the girl's parents, then leads her over to the campfire.

'Erin, this is my daughter, Mia,' she says, smiling at the teenager.

The girl looks older than Mia, probably sixteen if she has her L-plates. Mia hasn't seen her around, which is unusual in a place where everyone knows everyone. The nearby mine is putting on more staff, so maybe Erin's family are new to town.

Erin swats flies from her neat fringe and mutters, 'Hello.'

Her smile doesn't reach her eyes. It's hard to know

what to make of her. She has a stylish air about her, and her fitted jeans are tucked neatly into the most beautiful ankle boots Mia's ever seen.

'Hi.' Mia feels self-conscious as she scrapes mud off her own well-worn Blundstones. 'I'll go and get Bandit for you.'

Mia tucks wayward strands of hair behind her ears as she heads to where Bandit is waiting. She rests her head against the grey pony for a moment before taking a deep breath, then leads him back to the fire pit.

'This is Bandit,' Mia says brightly, trying to cover her awkwardness.

As Mum explains how to step into a stirrup and swing into the saddle, Mia holds Bandit's bridle, trying not to stare at Erin's nails. No wonder she struggled with the gate!

'It's okay.' Erin laughs. 'They're acrylic. It'd take more than a pony to break one.'

Mia blushes, embarrassed to have been caught staring.

'Make sure you behave yourself,' she whispers into Bandit's furry ear as Erin puts one boot in the stirrup.

Bandit harrumphs but stands steady.

'And this is how you hold the reins,' Mum explains.

Mia adjusts the stirrup length for Erin's long legs. Bandit is only fourteen hands high, so she's almost too tall for him.

'Ready?'

Erin nods.

'Walk on.' Mia leads Bandit around the training circle.

He flicks his head and Mia stops him to readjust the insect veil over the pony's eyes. The heat is already stifling and it's not even eight o'clock. The bureau is forecasting 38 degrees, but it feels like they've already passed that.

Erin's back is rigid. She's making a big effort to look relaxed, but Mia notices her pale knuckles gripping the reins.

'How are you doing?'

'Fine,' the older girl says curtly, arching an eyebrow.

Clearly not fine, Mia thinks. 'Have you ridden before?' she asks, holding the bridle firmly. Bandit can sense a rider's fear. He'll be mischievous if given half a chance.

'Yes, but that was on a *proper* bridle trail, not a dusty training circle.'

Mia struggles to keep her voice calm. 'Okay, let's leave the yard and you can ride around our short bush loop.' She pulls Bandit's head rope and they set off along the track, Biff padding along behind.

Despite Erin's attitude, Mia tries to be friendly as she walks alongside.

'You're doing well,' she says, even though Erin is yanking the bit in poor Bandit's mouth.

They head through typical Pilbara scrub, with spinifex grass and a few scraggly trees growing in the red pindan dirt. A mob of half-grown joeys hop towards them.

'They're our teenagers,' Mia tells the other girl, swishing flies from her face. Chatting usually helps riders

14

relax, so she continues trying to make conversation with Erin. 'Mum's vet speciality is horse care, but she treats injured wildlife as well. Our home is a madhouse.'

'I'd never seen wild kangaroos until we came to the Pilbara.'

'Really?' Mia tries to keep the surprise from her voice. She's never met anyone who hasn't seen roos hopping through the bush. Even Dad's buddies in Perth complain about them crossing roads on the outskirts of the city.

'We have a lot of other wildlife in Melbourne,' Erin adds defensively. 'Some outer suburbs have lyrebirds, wombats and even koalas. I just haven't seen kangaroos there.'

'Are you from Melbourne?'

'Yeah, we've moved here because my dad's on a short-term contract at Cape Lambert.'

'I'll bet the Pilbara is different to life over there.'

'It sure is!' Erin pouts. 'Dad's keen to make enough to pay off our boat, but if it wasn't for the money, I don't know why anyone would want to live here.'

Mia grips the halter, inwardly rolling her eyes.

'How can you stand this heat?' Erin continues. 'And the flies and dust and endless talk about possible cyclones . . . Wickham is *so* boring. There's nothing to do.'

'Have you been into Karratha?'

Erin pulls a face. 'It's not much better. The shops are terrible. In Melbourne my friends and I go shopping every weekend. It's what I miss most!'

'Did you see the Red Earth Arts Centre in Karratha?'

'Umm, yes!' Erin frowns, staring around at the wide

empty space. 'Dad says Melbourne has eighty times more people than *all* of the Pilbara.'

'Really?' Mia is surprised. Around 63 000 people live in the Pilbara; she can't imagine five million people in one place.

The older girl raises an eyebrow again. 'Mmhmm!' She gives Mia a withering smile, taps her boots against Bandit's belly and asks, 'Does this horse go any faster?'

If I slap his rump, Mia thinks, *he'll go fast enough to throw you*, but she bites back the words. Erin is a client. Besides, Bandit is being patient, and she doesn't want to slap his rump.

'We always take it easy on the first lesson.' Mia grits her teeth, then tries to be nice. 'I've never been to Melbourne. Or anywhere outside of WA!'

'You're joking!' Erin's voice is patronising. 'What about Perth?'

Mia nods. 'Most school holidays I fly down to the city to see my dad.'

Erin's posture loosens. Mia notices that as she relaxes, Erin begins swaying in time with Bandit's gait.

They're quiet for a while, then Mia says, 'I'm in Year Eight at West Pilbara High. What year are you? I haven't seen you on the school bus.'

'Year Ten – I'm sixteen. Dad's contract is only for three months, thank goodness, so I'm doing Distance Ed.'

'What's remote learning like?'

'It's all right.' Erin shrugs. 'But a bit hard to stay interested. Mum enrolled me in equine therapy so I'd meet other people around my age, and get outside more.'

Mia can't think of a reply. Most people come to Mum's sessions for more serious therapeutic reasons. She reminds herself not to be judgey.

'Our riders are mostly younger,' she tells Erin at last, 'and there aren't many teenagers between Wickham and Point Samson.'

'Seriously?' Erin glides her nails through her hair.

'On weekends, me and my friends go to Hatchling Cove,' Mia says. 'Have you been there?'

'Not yet.'

'It's only ten minutes' drive from Wickham. We'll be there this afternoon. I could introduce you to my friends.' Mia scuffs the dirt. 'We're only thirteen, but some of the older kids from school might be there.'

'Thanks.' Erin gives her a strange smile then looks away.

They reach the end of the circuit and Bandit stands quietly as Erin dismounts.

'Want to feed him?' Mia asks.

'Umm, sure.'

Mia hands Erin a carrot from the feed bucket. 'When Bandit is well behaved during a ride, we give him a treat.' She shows Erin how to hold her hand flat.

As Bandit nibbles the carrot Erin's smile seems genuine.

'His muzzle is so soft and whiskery!'

'It's lovely, isn't it?' Mia rests her head against Bandit's neck, then the pony turns to Erin and rubs his big, sweaty head across her beautiful clean shirt. Erin looks horrified.

'Sorry!' Mia stares at the horse slobber across Erin's chest. 'If you rinse your shirt as soon as you can, it should be okay.' She takes Bandit's halter and backs away.

'See you next week,' Mia calls, 'or maybe later at the beach.'

'Maybe.' Erin hurries across the yard to the waiting Land Rover.

'What's she like?' Mum asks as Mia leads Bandit back to the stables.

'Hmm, different to most people around here.'

When all the visitors have gone, Mia hoses down the horses. Biff jumps in and out of the horse trough. Then he shakes water over her with a contented doggy grin.

Mia laughs, wets her bandana and ties it around her neck. She can't wait to meet her friends at the beach and cool off properly. She grabs an orange from the kitchen, then heads to their wide veranda where the reception is best to text Kirra and Jess. She hopes they're in mobile range.

What time?

Two o'clock?

☺ ☺ ☺

The veranda faces south, so even on a hot day it's cool. Mia peels the orange and pops slices of fruit into her mouth, wondering who else'll be at Hatchling Cove. Being alone at the dugong end of the beach can still make her edgy, but today she'll be with her friends.

18

'Lunch, Mia.'

'Coming.'

'Did Erin enjoy her session with Bandit?' Mum asks, handing her a sandwich.

Mia shrugs. 'I think she expected white fences, polo shirts and a manicured track. She didn't like anything about our bush circuit, but she did like feeding Bandit, until he ruined her shirt.'

'What happened?'

Mia explains, then wolfs a sandwich and collects her snorkelling gear, hoping the snooty new girl won't be at her special beach.

Three

||||||||||||||||||||||||||||||||||||||||||||||||||||||||||||||||||||||||||||

They drive along their track, windows down, listening to Mia's favourite playlist. Mum turns left onto the Point Samson road, then cuts across to Walcott Drive.

As they cross a huge mining bridge, Mia looks down to watch an iron-ore train snaking through the scrub towards the 2.7 kilometre wharf at Cape Lambert. She's always amazed that a train, over a kilometre in length, can travel more than three hundred kilometres from the huge inland mine at Tom Price to the coast without a driver.

'It's weird to think that ore has come all the way from Tom Price.'

Mum glances down at the train. 'On Australia's largest private railway network.'

The scale of the Pilbara iron-ore industry is extraordinary. It's not just the trains that are autonomous; so are trucks and parts of the ports. Mia looks at the processing facility ahead.

'Imagine what we could do with all those billions of iron-ore dollars . . .'

Mum wipes her forehead. 'Fix the air con for a start. If the temperature gauge in the car is correct, we've just hit forty degrees.'

Mia winds up her window as Mum squirts water onto the windscreen and flicks the wipers. Everything around here is covered in iron-ore dust, and the difference between one side of Boat Beach Road and the other is startling. On the left side, sand dunes lead to sparkling waters teeming with sea-life; on the right, it's like a futuristic sci-fi movie setting. Massive machinery processes ore around the clock. A tall wire fence keeps the public out, but the fine dust escapes.

Mum leans forward to check the sky through the windscreen as they arrive at Hatchling Cove. All day, dense grey clouds have gathered, then scattered, then gathered again, as if they can't make up their minds what to do.

Hatchling Cove is beautiful in any weather. Waves break along the sheltered beach, shushing over pink-tinged sand, and a rustic yacht club, famous for Sunday fish and chips, perches on rocks above the carpark. Across the water in the distance, massive iron-ore ships wait to load up.

'I'll pick you up in two hours.' Mum pulls over where the beach meets the carpark. 'Or sooner if the rain starts.'

'Okay, or if Kirra's dad offers me a lift, I'll message to let you know.'

'Sounds good, darling – have fun.'

Mia drapes a towel across her shoulders and jogs down to the sand. She can't see the new girl, Erin, but there's a group of other senior students on the beach. As Mia approaches, one of them waves.

Mia waves back. 'Hi, Nick.'

She's known Nick as long as she's known Kirra – forever. Nick's sister came to equine sessions before she moved to a new school in Perth, and Nick used to help lead her horse around the yard.

From late December to mid-February, Mia and Nick volunteer with the local turtle monitoring program. They help researchers count hatchlings as they scamper down the beach. Mia loves being a hatchling monitor, helping to protect the turtles. Watching tiny flippers propel madly across the sand to the safety of the ocean is one of her favourite things in the world – up there with resting her head against Bandit's muzzle.

Chatting with Nick by torchlight on a pre-dawn nesting beach is easy, as he's so down-to-earth, but Mia feels self-conscious talking to him when he's with his friends. Some of those older kids are unapproachable. She hurries past and thinks about Bandit's warm muzzle.

'All okay,' she tells herself, 'it's all okay.'

'Miiiia!'

She squints into the distance. It's Kirra, swimming with their other bestie at the far end of the beach. Near where the dugong was.

Mia can't remember a time when she wasn't best friends with Kirra. They went to the same kindy, wrote notes to the tooth fairy together, built cubbies for Mum's rescue animals and drew cartoon figures on the local salt lake.

When they finish school, they both want to work with animals; Mia as a vet, and Kirra as a ranger. Kirra is endlessly fascinated by Mum's wildlife anecdotes. Nothing is too gross or embarrassing for her if it involves animals. Even when Mia's mum collects them from school with dried cow poo along her arms after cattle pregnancy testing, Kirra grins and wants to hear all the gory details.

Mia remembers the time in Year Five when her mum brought an ultrasound to school for show-and-tell. Mia was mortified as Mum explained each embarrassing step of artificial insemination and other reproduction details to the class, but Kirra loved it.

'Your mum is so cool,' she'd sighed while Mia groaned.

Their other friend, Jess, is newer to town. Her family works in the mining industry, and they moved from Perth to the Pilbara two years ago. Jess is fun and confident and loves anything to do with science, coming up with one brilliant idea after another. Jess nestled into their snug friendship quickly, and for the past two years they've been three wild musketeers, doing everything together. But lately the dynamics of their friendship seem to be changing . . .

'Come in,' Jess calls, 'the water is lovely.'

Mia throws her towel next to her friends' gear, avoiding looking at the high-tide line where the dugong died.

She runs over the burning sand and splashes through the waves. Kirra grabs Mia's legs, pretending to be a mythical kraken, just as she's done ever since they were six. They tumble down into the cooler water. Mia laughs as she escapes the imaginary cephalopod and comes up for air.

'I love Saturday afternoons with you guys,' she says.

The girls bob on the surface, chatting about school and what shows they're streaming. Mia floats on her back, basking in the cool water. Some days the ocean feels like a second home.

'A new girl came to horseriding this morning,' Mia tells her friends. 'She's over from Melbourne. I told her there'd be kids at the beach, so I thought she might be here.'

'Does she have long acrylic nails?' Kirra asks.

Mia nods, wondering when her friend became interested in fake nails.

'I saw her at the deli,' Kirra continues. 'She's tall, right?'

'Yes.'

'I love her clothes. I wanted to ask her where she got that shirt she was wearing.'

Probably a Melbourne boutique, Mia thinks.

They speculate a bit more about Erin, then swim to shore, re-sunblock and lie on their towels. Until the clouds darken and fat raindrops plop down from the sky.

'Here it comes again,' Jess mutters, wiping her glasses.

The girls gather their things and run to the carpark where Kirra's dad is waiting.

'Do you need a lift, Mia?'

'That'd be great.' She pulls out her phone to text her mum.

At home, Mum's busy rearranging boxes in her old vet surgery. It adjoins the lounge room and opens onto their veranda. Since Mum built her new vet office near the front gate, they use this room for storage and a quiet space for rescue wildlife, like Roxy, their tiniest rescue joey.

The frail, furless joey needs six bottles of formula every twenty-four hours, and a quick toileting lesson follows each feed. It's demanding work, but Mia and Mum love saving 'pinkies'. Mia wraps Roxy in a soft towel while she holds her tiny bottle steady. Even on hot Pilbara days, pinkies can't leave their pouch for long or they might catch a chill.

Her phone buzzes as she flops onto the couch. It's Dad on FaceTime.

'Hey, cara mia, how are you?'

Mia loves hearing Dad call her 'beloved' in his thick Italian accent.

'Bene, grazie.'

'That's good. What's happening in the north-west?' he asks.

'We started equine sessions this morning.'

'Already?'

'Yep, people were keen to begin riding, and it's not that long till the wet season ends.'

'Did your Bandit behave himself?'

'He did.' Mia plumps a cushion and stretches out.

'How are things in Perth? Are the twins behaving?' She hasn't visited Dad and her other family since mid-January. Last time they FaceTimed, the twins were cute, but feral.

'Everyone's fine.' He shifts the phone camera. 'Elena wants to ask you something.'

'Hi, Mia!'

Mia smiles, still feeling a little shy with her stepmum. Dad and Elena have been together three years, but Mia only sees Elena during holidays.

'I wanted to double-check your travel dates,' Elena says. 'We'd like to plan Tilda and Timmy's birthday party for when you're here.'

'But they don't turn two until May.'

'*We* know that.' Elena laughs. 'But they won't know if the celebration is a few weeks early, and we'd love you to share their special day.'

'Thank you.' Mia is touched.

'Thank *you*! It'll be good to have your backup. I have no idea what happens at two-year-old parties.'

'Lots of tantrums, in my experience,' Dad says, moving his face back into view.

'Ha, I'm sure I was an angel at two.'

'Of course you were!'

Mia checks the kitchen calendar. 'I'm flying down in five weeks, on Saturday the thirteenth.'

'That's perfect. We could have the party on Sunday, the day after you arrive.'

'I'll help organise things if you like.'

'Wonderful,' Elena replies. 'Thanks, Mia.'

'I'd better go.' Mia points to the kitchen. 'Mum's serving up chilli mussels.'

'We can't wait to see you.'

Dad blows Mia a kiss. 'Ciao, bambina.'

'That was nice of Elena,' Mum says after Mia ends the call.

'It was.' Mia slurps a spoonful of sauce, feeling grateful that her parents still get on okay.

After dinner they watch a movie. It's slow-moving and sentimental. Mum brushes Mia's hair as rain thrums on the corrugated tin roof.

They used to watch a lot of nature documentaries together before the dugong thing – David Attenborough was Mia's favourite wildlife warrior. Now she's more cautious. Images of climate-impacted animals can trigger nightmares like the one she had last night. Mia shivers, blocking that memory and Mum pauses halfway through twisting her hair into a bun.

'You all right?' she asks.

'Yep.' Mia takes a deep breath and unclenches her hands.

She reads a book in bed, and despite the rain, drifts into a deep sleep.

On Sunday Mia helps Mum sweep and paint her old surgery.

'Thanks.' Mum wipes her hands on her overalls. 'Once the paint dries we can organise dividing pens to separate the rescue animals.'

'It'll be good to get them out of the lounge.'

'It sure will.' Mum looks around the spacious lounge room. 'Lucky there's plenty of room in here.'

Late afternoon when the heat eases, they saddle Bandit and Sultan.

Mia ruffles Freckle's ears. 'Sorry you can't come with us today,' she tells the pony.

They trot to the end of their one-kilometre track, cross the main road, then canter along a bush path, circling the salt lakes until they come to their secret beach, not accessible by car.

Mia cheers as they gallop over rust-red dunes, her hair and Bandit's mane flying in the wind. They stop to catch their breath where the mudflats meet the sea.

'Imagine all those pearling luggers heading into Cossack in the eighteen-seventies,' Mum says, looking out to the lighthouse ruins on Jarman Island.

Mia pushes back her hair. Mum loves historical stories, while Mia prefers imagining what's below the waves.

She shades her eyes. Probably a few rays out there today. The tide is ebbing and salty rivulets slice the beach. Waves have contoured the mudflats, leaving shadowy patterns and textures.

'How can Erin not see the beauty here?' Mia asks Bandit, as sunlight silvers the ocean.

He snorts. A pair of sooty oystercatchers are running close to his hooves. Their long orange beaks probe the loosened mud searching for tiny crabs and molluscs.

'We'd better get back,' Mum calls.

Mia tongue-clicks and Bandit leaps forward, cantering home as dusk colours the spinifex. They follow a different track so they can pass the final resting area of Red Dog, the famous Pilbara kelpie.

At home Mum makes eggs on toast while Mia rubs down the horses. That night her sleep is peaceful again.

'Wake up, Mia, we're going to be late.'

Mia sits up. It's Monday morning and for once the corellas didn't wake her. She has a quick shower and puts on her school uniform. The pocket is decorated with their emblem: a Pilbara olive python, one of Australia's largest snakes. Some students reckon it's a creepy thing to have on a school shirt, but olive pythons aren't venomous and Mia likes them.

After finishing their chores, Mum drives Mia to the end of their track. They wait for the school bus, listening to an audio book – George Orwell's *Animal Farm*. They're up to chapter nine and poor old Boxer, the horse, is refusing to slow down, even though he's exhausted. Over the years they've listened to dozens of books during road trips or while they wait for the bus, but Mia reckons *Animal Farm* is one of the best.

When headlights appear, Mum says, 'Don't forget I'll be at the Karratha animal rescue centre this afternoon, so you don't have to catch the bus.'

Mia waves and steps onboard, carefully wiping her feet on Shazza's mud mat. Their purple-haired, caftanwearing driver roasts anyone who forgets. Mia sits in her usual spot and smiles at Nick in the seat behind.

'I thought you were getting your P-plates last week, and driving your dad's new four-wheel drive to school?'

'I'm doing the test after school today.'

'Good luck!' Mia throws her bag on the seat opposite, saving it for her friends, who'll get on in five minutes at Wickham.

Jaxon, a Year Ten guy, whispers something stupid from the seat behind and does his creepy hyena laugh. Nick narrows his eyes. 'If I get my licence, I won't miss the forty-five minute trip to Karratha with him!'

Shazza brakes suddenly and Mia braces, thinking how lucky Nick will be if he can borrow his dad's car for the long school commute. She wonders whether her mum will be as generous in a few years. Mia can't wait till she's old enough to get her licence. Mum's already started teaching her how to change gears and judge road distances.

At the Wickham turn-off, she stops daydreaming and grins at tourists taking selfies in front of the Haulpak, their local landmark. The giant yellow dump truck has become Instagrammable.

Kirra and Jess laugh as they jostle each other along the bus aisle towards Mia. Being in town, her friends get to spend more time together. They seem closer than ever this morning. She moves her bag, making room for them, and pushes away the strange left-out sensation washing over her. They dump their bags and flop onto the seats Mia has saved.

'We photobombed the tourists' photos!'

They fall about laughing, pretending to photobomb each other. Mia laughs too, but it feels a bit forced.

Shazza glares at them in the rear-view mirror, so Jess takes out her earphones and shares one with Kirra. They hum along to a song, but there's no third earphone. Mia turns back to the window, trying not to mind.

Their school is built from solid concrete blocks with sloping, cyclone-proof roofs and shade areas. There's a Japanese garden near the office with a red torii gate surrounded by plaques from mining partners. The landscaping around the rest of the school links to traditional plants and seasons. They walk past posters promoting Friday afternoon electives. Jess wants them all to do robotics, but Mia thinks spinifex basket-weaving sounds fun.

In English, their teacher gives them a new assignment.

'I want each of you to choose a complex issue and write a short persuasive piece,' Ms Malouf tells them. 'After showing me a draft, you'll need to practise reading it before presenting the piece as a speech to the class.'

What? Mia feels her hands become clammy.

'How long should the persuasive speech be?' Jess asks.

'Between four and five minutes. Marks will be deducted if it's too long or too short.'

Jess is grinning. She's the school's star debater and loves this kind of thing. Meanwhile, Mia dreads the idea of speaking in front of the class, let alone talking persuasively. She's passionate about plenty of issues, but building an argument from one viewpoint is tricky. Mia has a habit of seeing both sides of things. It's so frustrating.

'Just pick a topic,' Jess tells her during the bus ride home, 'choose a position and stick with it.'

'It's all right for you!'

Jess is forever watching TEDx talks online. She's already written a list of possible topics.

'What are you going to talk about?' Mia asks Kirra, looking for inspiration.

'Animal cruelty. I think I'll argue against caged hen farming and for stricter policing of free-range egg operators.'

Jess turns to Mia. 'You could do animal cruelty too,' she suggests. 'What about those brumbies they're shooting? Or dumping ex-racehorses like Sultan in the bush? You often talk about that.'

'Hmm.' Mia can't decide. She cares about brumbies and rescue horses, but if she has to stand in front of thirty people and talk, she wants to choose something everyone can relate to. Maybe she could talk about climate change or some aspect of that, like human threats to marine life. The net-tangled dugong comes to mind, and she shudders, then takes a breath.

She mightn't be ready to talk about *dugongs* yet, but she could speak about conservation, and how even small actions can help fragile environments.

After that first panic attack, Mum took her to a counsellor.

'I know you're worried,' Mum said as they sat in the waiting room. 'I'm not sure how to help, but it will be good to talk to someone who can.'

The counsellor taught Mia about mindfulness,

breathing and sensory techniques, like focusing on things she can hear or smell. She learned that doing practical things is empowering. Now, when Mia feels overwhelmed, knowing *she* can make a difference makes her feel stronger.

As the bus pulls up at Wickham, Mia wonders whether climate action is a good topic for her talk.

By the time she gets home, Mia's more confused than ever. *Stop overthinking it*, she tells herself, *and pick something!*

Four

Day after day, wet season cloud monsters fill the sky, forming and reforming in enormous, looming shapes. Mia wonders whether any will build into a cyclone. The dark clouds gather in the late afternoon, before a short, heavy downpour, and then blow away. She loves the dramatic lightning shows, but not the relentless wet season heat.

The vet surgery is busy. After school on Thursday, Mia helps Mum treat a cat with a huge dental abscess. The old moggy needs a general anaesthetic before they can put a drain in place. Mia watches as Mum carefully sterilises her equipment, then she holds the cat steady while Mum finds the best vein. Surgical work fascinates Mia. Her long-term dream is to work beside Mum as a fully qualified animal surgeon.

On Saturday morning, Rosa turns up, despite the stormy sky and drizzling rain.

'Mum, gone,' Mia tells her in stilted Auslan, then fingerspells *Wickham*.

'I know,' Rosa signs back. 'Dad says it's too dangerous for riding today, but can I brush Sultan, or sit with him?'

Mia hesitates. Their clients know Mum cancels equine therapy during thunderstorms, but Rosa looks so sad and bedraggled.

'Please?' Rosa adds, while her father shrugs an apology.

'Okay,' Mia replies, remembering herself a few years back, when she was just as horse-mad. 'Sultan would love that.'

Rosa high-fives her dad.

'Is it all right if I wait here on the veranda?' he asks, tapping a passcode into his phone. 'I need to answer some emails.'

'Sure.'

Mia grabs her English assignment notes and they race through the rain to the stable. Sultan snorts in delight when he sees his little friend. Rosa plaits Sultan's mane while Mia leans against Bandit's stall, reviewing ideas for her speech.

Talking about dumped racehorses would make her too emotional. She crosses that out. Culling brumbies by helicopter would also be a hard topic. Mia hates aerial shooting, but relocating wild horses is slow, and gelding the stallions is expensive. Brumby hooves damage fragile ecosystems, and their numbers need to be controlled, but with aerial culling wounded horses can die slowly instead of being killed outright. Mia crosses out that idea as well. It would take longer than five minutes to try to untangle all sides of that emotive debate.

She chews her lip, thinking about turtle hatchlings scuttling down the beach after they've broken free from their shells. Global warming has threatened their chances of survival in so many ways. Mia taps her pen against a knee. Hatchlings face threats, not only from introduced cats, foxes and other predators, but also from other human-caused problems: net tangle, dune erosion, turtle-shell trade, microplastics and warming ocean currents. Raising awareness for hatchlings is a strong topic if she can just find a way to shape it.

Ms Malouf said to choose something you're passionate about, and to balance that passion with reason. Mia loves horses, but helping turtles is her passion. After hours of monitoring hatchlings, it's also something she knows about. And if she needs scientific references, or facts and figures, Nick's dad might be able to help. He takes marine biologists and scientists through the mangroves on his charter boat and out to nesting beaches in the Dampier Archipelago.

For the first time since Ms Malouf gave them the assignment, Mia feels excited to get started. She gathers her thoughts and smiles at Rosa polishing Sultan's hind hooves. That kid is fearless.

'Great job,' she signs, but Rosa doesn't notice. She's in her own horsey heaven. And if Sultan was a cat, he'd be purring.

Mia writes dot points into an outline, then realises she has way too many points for a five-minute speech. Ms Malouf told them to be specific. Mia starts a new page. Which turtle threat should she focus on?

A delicious smell of fresh damper drifts towards them. That *does* make Rosa look up.

'Hi, Jimmee,' she calls.

The silver-haired stockman has parked his ute by the gate and is hobbling across the yard. He gives Rosa a nod, 'Glad there's *someone* here to enjoy a feed.' He hangs his Driza-Bone coat on a hook. 'Where are the rest of 'em – scared off by a few drops of rain?'

Mia looks beyond the stable. The clouds are building and the 'drops of rain' are already forming puddles on the ground.

Jimmy hands them each a chunk of warm damper, a knife and the jam jar, then pours three mugs of tea from a thermos. They slather mango jam over the bread and listen to the steady rain and nickering of horses.

'I love your damper,' Rosa signs, and presses her arms across her chest, smiling.

Jimmy winks, not needing an interpreter to work that out. He offers her another piece, then peers at the sky. 'I reckon this storm could blow into a cyclone,' he says. 'Most of the corellas have shot through.'

Mia looks over at the roosting tree. 'I thought it was quiet.' She pats Biff. 'Hey buddy, no birds for you to chase today!'

'And see here.' Jimmy points to the wooden beams where highways of ants are moving their eggs to higher ground.

'Don't they shift their eggs every time there's a storm?'

'Not that high, unless it's a big one.' Jimmy strokes

his beard. 'Those little white things they're carrying are pupas – cocoons that are almost ready to hatch. The adult ants have to protect them.' He chuckles at Mia's surprised face. 'I never finished school, but Mother Nature is the best teacher. Those ants are tiny, but they know a thing or two about barometric pressure.'

'I haven't heard a warning on the radio,' Mia says as thunder rumbles through the sky.

Jimmy shrugs. 'I put my faith in bush creatures ahead of those boffins at the weather bureau.'

Mia remembers the first time she asked Jimmy why he doesn't have wi-fi or a mobile phone.

'Don't need it,' he'd replied. 'After living out bush all me life, I've got a sixth sense, like the birds and animals. They tell me what's happening.' He'd winked and Mia still doesn't know whether he was joking.

Sheet lightning glows in the darkening clouds. Rosa's dad looks up from his phone on the veranda and waves. Rosa pretends not to notice. He waves again, tapping his watch. Mia tries to sign, 'I don't mind if she stays a bit longer,' but as she flicks her fingers awkwardly, Rosa laughs.

'Did I do that wrong?' Mia asks.

Rosa nods and repeats the correct message. Mia wonders what she'd signed instead.

A sudden gust of wind rattles the roof. The spooked horses snort and Freckles stamps her hooves.

'Might be time for me to skedaddle.' Jimmy gathers his coat. 'Let's hope I'm wrong and this weather clears.'

'Me too,' Rosa signs. They tidy up, then race across

the yard to the veranda. 'Thank you,' Rosa calls, blowing a kiss as she gets into the car.

'You're welcome,' Mia signs.

Mum returns from town with more groceries than usual.

'Just in case this weather keeps building,' she says.

Mia helps prepare tacos for lunch, then in the afternoon, she works on her sea-glass jewellery.

Once the cyclone season ends, travellers will start heading north, and Mia's making a stack of jewellery to sell at the Karratha Mothers' Day Market. Half the money she raises will go to the local animal rescue organisation. The other half is for buying a new set of headphones. If enough tourists turn up, she'll sell everything she's made. In the meantime Mia's been working on a new earring design.

'What do you think?' she asks Mum.

'I'll buy a pair. I love the way you recycle beach junk into beautiful things.'

Mia laughs. Mum is her best customer!

She spreads her sea-glass across the table, arranging fragments into matching shapes and colours. Soon she'll need more pieces. Mia finds weathered glass at Point Samson, on the tip of the peninsula. White and green glass washes up most often. Blue is harder to find, but that's the colour tourists like best.

Mia collects the shards that are too small for earrings and arranges them into a star shape. She wonders how they'd look on a bridle, or on the flap of a leather saddle-bag. Maybe she could use sea-glass to decorate horse gear, or glue tiny fragments onto boots like Rosa's. Rodeo riders love bling.

'Hey, Mum,' Mia calls, 'I've got a new idea!'

A short, heavy downpour interrupts her words.

Mia spends the rest of the rainy weekend texting her friends and researching and writing her English assignment. She reads about the record-breaking marine heatwave along the West Australian coast in 2011 when the water temperature reached five degrees warmer than usual. There was unprecedented coral bleaching. Marine ecosystems were devastated.

The more Mia researches marine pollution and warming oceans, the more anxious she becomes.

'Breathe,' she tells herself. 'Being aware is the first step . . .'

One trick the counsellor taught her was to mind-list five things she can see, four things she can hear, three things she can touch and two things she can smell. That helps centre her thoughts.

Last year Mia also started a gratitude journal. She closes her eyes for a moment and feels grateful that Biff is resting his head on her foot, then she returns to those hatchling problems . . .

Most people know about the dangers of ghost nets and microplastic, but not many people know that climate change alters sand temperature which can affect the sex of hatchlings, or that rising sea levels are flooding turtle nesting areas. Her speech could focus on those things.

Mia drafts an opening sentence:

Each year the Leeuwin Current sweeps down Australia's west coast, bringing tropical water and raising the ocean temperatures.

Hmm, not very catchy. She tries again.

Turtle hatchlings return to the beach where they hatched to lay their eggs as adults, but erosion from rising sea levels and increased storm surges are destroying many nesting sites.

Mia sighs and takes a break.

'What do *you* think about helping hatchlings?' she asks Roxy, their furless pinkie, as she lifts the joey out of her flannelette pouch. Roxy wriggles. 'Yes, I know,' Mia strokes her ears. 'As long as you get your regular feeds, you don't care.'

She holds the joey's bottle in one hand and sends a text to Kirra and Jess with the other.

What r u doing?

Nothing!

As they send messages back and forth, Mia tells them she's decided to do her talk on human threats to turtle hatchlings.

Great choice.

Including microplastic?

👍 Yes, and rising seas flooding turtle nests, and the feminisation of hatchlings.

What!!

Warmer sand means more female hatchlings. It's a huge problem.

☹ I didn't know that. . .

They swap ideas and other gossip until Mum calls out, 'Have you finished your homework?'

'Almost.'

Have to go . . .

Mia hangs Roxy's pouch in the old surgery, then adds another paragraph to her speech, making detailed notes about microplastic. Then she opens her gratitude journal and draws an image of herself texting messages to her friends. She keeps the image in mind as she switches off the light, hoping it will keep nightmares at bay.

Five

||||||||||||||||||||||||||||||||||||||||||||||||||||||||||||||||||||||||||||

Rain beats over the tin roof and by morning the puddles are interconnected ponds. Mia wakes early. There were no nightmares. Her gratitude image worked! She reads for a while, then paces her room, sick of being cooped up inside.

The lightning show has passed, leaving oppressive heat and drizzle that soaks Mia as she splashes across to the stable to feed the horses. Bandit snuggles up, hoping for a carrot.

'Hello, everyone!'

Mia fills the horses' feed troughs and slaps bugs as she clears manure. The steamy conditions are fiesta time for insects.

After chores and breakfast, Mum drives her to the bus stop. Headlights appear through the steamy mist and Mia pulls on her raincoat, ready to make a dash when Shazza stops.

'I'll head into Karratha after morning surgery,' Mum reminds her. 'The rescue centre has new animals, so I'll check them out, then pick you up around three o'clock. Or earlier if this weather gets worse. Jimmy's convinced that a cyclone's brewing.'

'It might track up towards Hedland again,' Mia says, 'or not even make landfall.'

'Let's hope so!' Mum replies, 'but our barometer *is* dropping . . .'

Mia jumps a puddle and steps onto the bus. She wipes her feet on Shazza's mud mat, then walks towards her usual seat. Nick is in the seat behind, sitting next to creepy Jaxon.

'What are you doing back on the bus?' she asks.

'Dad won't let me drive today,' Nick replies. 'He reckons I need more experience before taking his new four-wheel drive out in a cyclone.'

'Fair call, but it's not actually a cyclone.'

'Not yet.'

Living in the heart of Western Australia's 'cyclone alley', they're all used to guessing which of the wet season storms will become a cyclone. Fewer than half of them meet land.

'Dad thinks this one will cross near us,' Nick says. 'The fish have stopped biting. They often go quiet before a big blow.'

'And the corellas have flown inland. Jimmy reckons they know when a cyclone's coming.'

'I hope our hatchlings are well out to sea.' Nick gives Mia a worried glance. 'If this *does* build and the eye crosses at high tide, sea surge will flood the nests.'

'All those clutches must have hatched by now . . .'

'Yeah, I s'pose you're right. It's weeks since our last callout. Fingers crossed there are no stragglers.'

'The storm is probably just another fizzer,' Jaxon scoffs.

'Hope so.' Nick's eyes twinkle at Mia. 'Then I can drive Dad's car tomorrow.'

Mia grins and wipes the foggy window, but it clouds immediately in the steamy air. Not being able to see out feels weird.

'Too much heavy breathing,' hyena-boy whispers.

Mia ignores him as Nick says, 'The glass was already fogged when we left Point Samson.'

'Is your dad chartering the boat today?'

Nick nods. 'He's going out with an international mangrove specialist this morning, but they'll stay close to shore. I wanted to help, but Dad said I need to be at school.' He frowns. 'The whole point of me staying at school is to study marine biology. I may as well get some early practice when I can.'

'He wants you to do well in your exams.'

'I know.' Nick sighs.

'With a big-paying mine on our doorstep,' Jaxon mutters, 'only losers go away to uni.'

As Jaxon cackles at his own comment, Nick raises an eyebrow at Mia.

'What?' He juts out his chin. 'Once an apprenticeship comes up, I'm out of school. This time next year I could be earning big bucks, with a deposit on a car and leftover cash to hire Nicko here to take me out on fishing trips.'

Nick laughs. 'In your dreams.'

'At least you're both nearly finished.' Mia pulls a face. 'I've still got *years* on the school bus before I even begin studying vet science. *If* my marks are high enough to get into uni!'

'They will be.' Nick smiles at her, then stares out at the moody-looking sky. 'Dad also had an afternoon fishing trip booked to Bezout Island, but they cancelled.'

'Because of the weather?'

'Yep, maybe it's for the best. Dad's been so busy.'

'Busy is good, isn't it?'

'Good for paying off the boat, but his dodgy shoulder is getting worse. With Mum away in Perth, he needs more help with the business.'

'Your mum used to go out on the boat with him before she went to Perth, hey?'

'Yeah, we're counting the days till she and Lexi come home for school holidays.'

'How's Lexi's new school?' Mia asks.

'She loves it. Mum says her teacher has designed a work program around what she *can* do, not what she can't do.'

'I'm really glad.'

'Me too.' Nick's quiet for a moment then he says, 'Jeez, I'd have loved to spend the morning with that mangrove scientist—'

Shazza brakes suddenly.

'Whoa,' everyone yells.

'Bloody bitumen-hogging road train!' Shazza swears as the bus splashes into a deep puddle on the verge.

Mia hears the little kids at the front laugh and repeat, 'Bloody road train.'

Shazza's a rough Pilbara diamond. She's driven most of them to school since kindy and Mia's heard a lot worse from her over the years.

'Sorry,' Shazza shouts, regaining control of the bus. 'Don't tell your parents that I swore again!'

The little kids giggle, reminding Mia of her siblings in Perth. She pictures their chubby toddler legs galloping along Dad's hallway. Timmy and Tilda are gorgeous, but they're full-on bundles of energy. Mia wonders what it would be like living with the twins in Perth for five years while she studies. Could she manage city life for that long? What about her panic attacks? She's never really spoken to her dad about them.

If she does get into vet school, it will be strange doing the reverse to now; living with Dad and coming back to Mum for holidays.

Mia tucks a strand of loose hair into her ponytail. Flying over a thousand kilometres south to stay with Dad, Elena and the twins is fun during school holidays, but after a week she's ready to come home. Staying in the Pilbara to study vet science would be perfect, but the nearest uni is a sixteen-hour drive away.

Shazza stops at the Wickham turn-off and Mia wipes the window. There are no tourists in front of the giant Haulpak today. The rain has scared them away. She watches her friends run to the bus. They're sharing an umbrella, splashing through puddles and laughing together. The left-out feeling washes over her again as they dump their bags and flop onto the seats Mia has saved.

'We're soaked!'

'You are!'

'And look.' They hold out their hands. 'We found out where that new girl had her nails done. So yesterday we got ours painted in Wickham footy colours.'

Wow, Mia thinks, *I didn't see that coming!* She turns back to the window and chews on one of her own chipped nails. Since when did Kirra and Jess start doing their nails? Since Erin arrived!

Shazza parks behind a line of other buses. Only the Karratha town kids walk to school. They arrive early and hang around the lockers until the siren sounds, looking cooler than everyone else.

Jess is in advanced mathematics, so Kirra and Mia sit together in general maths. Mia is glad to have her friend's full attention, but she can't stop staring at Kirra's nails. When Mr Finch asks her to answer a question, Mia stumbles, embarrassed to be caught not paying attention. She looks at her teacher blankly, trying to think of something to say, until Mr Finch calls on someone else.

The rain continues all day. In every class, teachers hand out the school's cyclone policy and remind them how to stay safe during a cyclone.

'During a Blue Alert school will stay open,' they say, 'but if we get to a Yellow Alert you need to stay home.'

'What about if it's Red?' someone asks.

'Take shelter!'

After school Mia waves goodbye to her friends, then races through the carpark to where Mum's van is waiting.

'Looks like another false alarm,' Mia says, jumping in. 'Mr Finch told us the tropical low bringing all this weather is still off the coast, hundreds of kilometres away.'

'I don't know.' Mum hands Mia a smoothie in her help-the-turtles keep cup. 'Jimmy's instincts are usually spot on. When we get home let's secure everything in the yard. Better safe than sorry.'

'Okay.' Mia takes a sip of smoothie. 'How many new animals today?'

'Just three kittens. They're covered in a nasty rash, but otherwise healthy.'

Every Monday afternoon, when Mum isn't delivering a foal or working at a cattle station, she visits the SAFE animal shelter to treat new arrivals. If the shelter is overflowing, they sometimes become temporary dog carers. And then some of their 'temporary' pets, like Biff the kelpie, never leave. They don't take kittens in case they escape. There are already way too many feral cats in the Pilbara.

'Indian or Thai for dinner?' Mum asks.

'Indian, please!'

For Mia, the best thing about Rescue Shelter Mondays is buying takeaway dinner.

They drive home and Mum stacks their garden furniture in the shed while Mia grabs a shovel and digs a channel around the stable. She needs to steer water away from the building before it weakens the footings.

Before long, Mia's soaked, but the weather is stifling so it's kind of fun. Her last job is feeding the horses.

'Sorry, guys,' she tells them, loading hay and a handful of grains into their feed troughs, 'you can't go out for a run this evening.'

They nicker and Bandit nudges her leg. Mia presses her face against his soft neck until Freckles suddenly shrieks. Their smallest horse is more dependable than a watchdog. Mia looks up. A car is at the gate.

Someone arriving unexpectedly usually means an animal emergency. Mia runs out to unloop the chain. It's Sharpie, another of their neighbours.

'Thank goodness you're home.' Sharpie's voice is strangely high as he points to his terrier in the back seat. 'I think Chilli's been bitten by a snake.'

Mum must have also heard the car, because she's standing on the veranda.

'Snakebite,' Mia yells, wiggling her arm as a signal in case Mum can't hear her above the rain.

'Take Chilli into Mum's surgery,' Mia tells Sharpie, pointing to the little building by the stable, then she relatches the gate and runs after the car.

Mum is already crossing the yard.

'What kind of snake?' she asks as Sharpie cradles Chilli.

'Maybe a western brown. I only saw the tail . . .'

'You sure it wasn't a lizard?

'Positive.'

Mia hopes it wasn't a king brown, or worse, a death adder. During heavy rain, snakes sometimes leave their

50

burrows and slither into buildings. Jimmy told her that one rainy night an orange-naped snake surprised him in the outhouse. Luckily he saw it in time.

Chilli shudders, then pees on the examination table, both signs of snakebite.

'Do you want me to give her antivenom?'

'Of course! I don't care how much it costs, she's me best mate.'

'I know, Sharpie, but I have to ask.'

Antivenom costs a bomb, and Mia knows that if the poison has already taken hold, the treatment might not work. Some owners decide to let an old animal go rather than pay hundreds of dollars.

As Mum prepares an IV drip and takes serum from the vet surgery fridge, Mia wipes the table and lays a fresh towel under the terrier.

'Thanks.' Sharpie blinks back tears. He's one of the toughest guys in town, but Chilli is his princess. Sharpie owns the tattoo parlour in Wickham, and loves Jack Russell terriers so much that he does tatts of them for free. Half the port workers have Chilli's face inked somewhere on their body.

Sharpie turns his face away as Mum finds a vein and inserts the drip.

'Would you like a cuppa?' Mia taps his arm.

'That'd be beaut, love, it might settle me nerves.'

'Tea or coffee?'

'Either.'

Mia brews a pot of coffee as Mum fits an oxygen mask to calm the terrier before injecting serum. After a few minutes, Chilli's ragged breathing settles and her muscle spasms ease.

'Looks like you got here in time,' Mum says, stroking Chilli's chest.

'Thank goodness.' Sharpie flops onto a chair. 'And lucky the cops didn't see me tearing up the main road.'

'They might have given you a police escort!' Mia hands him a mug of strong coffee. 'Everyone loves Chilli.'

'Ha ha, that'd be something old Banksy would have done before he retired, but I can't see that new sergeant turning on the siren for a dog.'

Mum settles Chilli in a towel-lined cage and tells Sharpie that she'd like to keep the terrier overnight for observation.

'I'll need to flush Chilli's kidneys and check her urine. If it's red, we'll know there's still venom in her system.' Mum peers out at the moody sky. 'Given the weather, we'll keep her with us at the house. How about I call later this evening and give you an update?'

'Thanks, Doc. Let me know how much I owe you and I'll bring cash tomorrow.' Sharpie pauses. 'And if you ladies ever want a Jack Russell tattoo, complimentary of course, you know where to come.'

'Cheers, Sharpie.' Mum laughs. 'I think we're good for now.'

Six

||||||||||||||||||||||||||||||||||||||||||||||||||||||||||||||||||||||||||||||

Mia is used to cyclone build-ups, but the noise and energy of the wild rain squalls keeps her awake half the night. It's a relief when she hears Chilli scratching at her cage at dawn. She gets up to check the terrier.

'How's her temperature?' Mum calls from the next room.

'Normal.'

'Thanks for getting up to check. Her temp was still a little high when I gave Roxy her two a.m. bottle.'

Mia takes the terrier outside and waits for her to sniff out a good place to do her business. She tucks Chilli back into the cage, then sits on Mum's bed to listen to a radio weather update. Besides flood warnings, no other alerts have been issued. That means she still has to go to school!

Mia goes back to her room, sits on her bed and chews the end of a pen. She'll have to think of something else to add to her gratitude journal.

After writing *I'm grateful Chilli survived the snakebite*

Mia downloads some new music. They eat breakfast, then she grabs her bag and they drive up the track in pouring rain to wait for the bus.

At school the corridors are half-empty. So are Mia's classes.

'How come our parents didn't let us stay at home?' Jess complains as she cleans her glasses.

Mia and Kirra shrug.

They use their double-English period to help each other practise their persuasive talks. Jess has prepared two speech outlines – one debating the gender pay gap in sport and another arguing for an operational Emissions Trading Scheme.

'I wish I could do both,' she sighs.

Mia shakes her head in disbelief.

When they show their drafts to Ms Malouf, she says, 'These look good. I'm looking forward to hearing you present them.'

At recess they sit in the undercover area as a weird mist settles over the oval. Then, in History, they watch a slideshow with images of the nearby Burrup rock art.

'The petroglyphs are tens of thousands of years old,' their teacher says. 'Some of the images show Tasmanian devils and thylacine, both extinct on the mainland. The carvings are a sacred place for traditional owners . . .'

Mia gazes out the window, remembering the hallowed feeling of walking through those engraved rocks, similar to the stillness of Hamersley Gorge at Karajini, or inside the cathedral at Geraldton. But the petroglyphs sit alongside massive mining development.

'The Burrup Peninsula was an island,' their teacher continues, 'until the nineteen-sixties when industry built a road and rail causeway.' Mia stares out the window, imagining the area back when it was an island.

Jess puts up her hand and asks, 'Are chemicals and mine dust damaging the rock art?'

'That's a great research question for this week's homework . . .'

After school, Shazza is wearing a new psychedelic caftan with matching butterfly clips in her hair. She grins when Mia admires the clips, then eases them through an armada of school buses.

As they drive north along the highway, Jess and Kirra share earphones again. Mia wipes the window, looking out and trying to think of something to be grateful for to stop feeling anxious about their friendship. The rain and humidity have cooked up a fog so thick that she can barely see the giant three-armed electrical towers straddling the flat countryside like weird space creatures.

The mist reminds Mia of cooler July mornings when she grooms the horses and their breath puffs from their nostrils in little clouds. She smiles and rests her head on the glass window, breathing deeply.

A vehicle is flashing its headlights at the Wickham turn-off. It looks like Mum's vet van. Wickham is one stop before Mia's regular drop-off. *What's she doing here?* Mia gets off the bus with Jess and Kirra, the wind pushing them against each other.

'Hi, Mum, is everything all right? How come you're waiting here?'

'The shire has set up a sandbagging depot on the footy oval.'

'Oh no.' Mia groans, guessing what's coming next.

Annual flooding is part of life in the Pilbara. When the weather forecasters announce *heavy rain which may inundate low-lying areas and spread quickly*, Mia knows shovelling sand will be involved.

Even if this tropical low doesn't build into a cyclone, slow systems like this can cause flooding across the Pilbara. Every wet season, communities organise truck-loads of sand for locals to bag up and protect their buildings.

'I'll help,' Kirra offers. Her home is built on a high pad which rarely floods.

Jess flexes her arms. 'Me too. I need to build up my biceps.'

'Thanks, girls!' As Mum drives them all to the oval, Mia gives her friends a grateful smile. *Stop worrying*, she tells herself, *we're all okay*.

Mum hands out hessian bags, gloves, a bucket and shovels from the back of the car. The bucket is open at both ends.

'What's this bottomless bucket for?' Jess pushes her glasses further onto her nose.

'Put it onto the top of that hessian bag.' Mum shows Jess how the bucket keeps the bag open, making it easier to shovel.

'Brilliant. I love practical inventions like this.'

Kirra and Jess use the bucket option while Mia helps Mum.

'Only fill to two-thirds,' Mum reminds her, 'or the bag will be too heavy to lift.'

Mia takes care to bend her knees. Vets who work with large animals need to look after their backs.

Dozens of other Wickham families are also out sandbagging. Everyone is soaked, but no one seems to mind.

'How's your foal coming along?' Mum asks one young woman.

'Gypsy is growing so quickly.' The woman opens her phone and taps on a photo. 'Look.'

Mum smiles. 'She's beautiful.'

They fill another bag, then an older man leads his dog towards Mum.

'Hello, Blue.' She pats the ancient heeler and checks his ears and teeth. 'You're looking well.'

'Thanks to you, Zara.' The old man winks.

Unlike some of the fly-in fly-out towns across the Pilbara, Wickham and Point Samson have mostly permanent residents. Mia likes being part of a small close community where people know each other and help out at times like this.

Mia sees the new girl crossing the oval.

'How weird is this?' Erin shouts, splashing towards them as she balances a takeaway coffee. 'I've never sandbagged before.'

'This is Erin,' Mia tells her friends reluctantly. 'She's from Melbourne and it's her first wet season.'

'I love your jeans,' Jess yells into the rain.

'Thanks.' Erin tucks flying strands of hair back into her French braid. 'I can't believe this wind!'

Mia notices that Erin is wearing designer runners instead of her expensive boots.

'Erin came to Mum's equine therapy sessions last Saturday,' Mia tells her friends.

'Mum made me.' Erin looks uncomfortable. 'I'm not normally anxious, or into "therapy".' She glances at Mia and gives her a fake smile. 'I just don't know many people here yet.'

'Where do you live?' Jess asks.

'A block behind the bistro.'

'That's near me.' Jess beams. 'And Kirra is only two streets away. Maybe we could hang out sometimes.'

Erin runs her fingers through her fringe. Hair fans across her forehead and her nails sparkle in the stormy light. 'That sounds great.'

Something about the energy of pre-cyclone weather makes people giddy and silly and light-headed. As they keep digging, Mia shouts above the wind, 'The shovel is such a great invention, it's truly groundbreaking.'

'Wow, that's a really bad joke!' Erin mutters, avoiding eye contact with Mia before grinning at Jess and Kirra for support.

Mia does wriggly wet cephalopod arms at Kirra in reply, but her friend looks away, as though embarrassed. 'I think we're getting too old for that?' Kirra whispers, glancing at Erin. The older girl smirks.

Mia drops her arms and looks away, feeling betrayed.

The rain keeps drizzling down. As Erin runs back

to help her parents, fierce gusts lash the oval, knocking over the sandbagging sign. Volunteers try to weigh it down, but the gusts are too strong. They give up and start folding it away.

'That wind's not easing,' Mum yells. 'I reckon the bureau might call it soon. Thanks for your help, girls. We have enough bags now. Let's tie the tops to transport them.'

They load the sandbags into the car. Mia feels confused as Mum drops Kirra and Jess at their homes. Only days ago at the beach, Kirra loved cephalopod impersonations. What's changed?

They drive out of town with the windscreen wipers going full pelt. Mia doesn't feel like talking, so she's glad when Mum turns up the radio. There's *still* no cyclone warning.

A broad-winged kite circles in the rain. As they turn off the main road, the bird darts to the ground, rising with a small creature struggling in its hooked talons. Mia turns away, feeling a little like prey herself.

At home she feeds the joeys and horses, trying not to think about Erin, Jess and Kirra. Mia helps Mum lay thick plastic around the vet surgery, then they drag sandbags onto the plastic, making a flood barrier. Mum wears a brace to support her lower back and Mia helps stack the heavy bags like brickwork, with the now-open top part of each bag covered by its neighbour. They build two layers outside, letting the bags settle into place, before adding another layer inside the door.

'Okay,' Mum says, 'that should do. Whatever happens now, we're well prepared.'

After dinner Mia reads her speech, then stretches out on the couch. The wi-fi is dropping in and out, so she gives up on social media and reads her library book instead. Then the landline rings.

Mia picks up the phone. 'Hello, this is Pilbara Animal Care. Can I help you?'

'Hi, Mia, it's Jude from Spinifex Downs. How's the wind over there?'

'Wild!'

'Same here.'

'How are your brumbies?' Mia pushes the speaker phone button so she can hear better over the whistling wind.

'Not too bad, thanks. I need to talk to your mum. Is she there?'

'Mum's checking the joeys. Hold on, I'll go and get her.'

'Thanks, Mia.'

Mum and Jude chat briefly about the storm and the possibility of it building into a cyclone. Because of the speaker phone Mia can't help but overhear their conversation.

'So what's happening, Jude?'

'Our new mare, Raven, is acting strangely.'

'The expensive one?'

'That's right. Remember how I told you she was putting on weight? Well, this week, our fears were realised – she's started pacing and lying down more often than usual.'

'Has Raven been near your stallion?' Mum asks.

'No, we've kept him well away.'

'Could she have met one of the wild horses?'

'We didn't think so, but Dave saw brumby stallions hanging around the water pipeline last year.'

'Do you remember *when* he saw them?'

'Around Easter, eleven months ago, so I guess an unplanned pregnancy is possible.'

'How do her udders look?'

'Rounder than usual.'

'Hmm, it sounds like she could be getting ready to foal.'

'That's what we're afraid of. Dave's ropeable. He reckons he didn't spend a fortune buying a stock-horse with Raven's bloodline to risk her life on an early pregnancy.'

'She's a special mare—'

'Twenty-five thousand dollars of special! I've never seen a better campdrafter. The way Raven separates cattle from a mob and yards a beast is instinctive. She barely needs direction from me.' Jude pauses. 'We have such big plans for her.'

'I remember you telling me how the prize-money from Raven's wins will help rehome brumbies – what an amazing initiative.'

'Or truck several rescue racehorses to Perth,' Jude says. 'It's not many animals in the scheme of things, but every horse we save counts.'

'It sure does. I've got Sultan to remind me of that every day. So, what can I do to help?'

'The weather's foul, but I don't suppose you could

come and check her? If we lose Raven, Dave will be gutted. He's never spent this much on a horse and we've both grown to love her.'

Mum looks out the window into the rain. 'How about you keep Raven inside tonight,' she suggests. 'If you take observations every few hours, I'll call early tomorrow morning to hear how she's progressing. In the meantime, I'll make sure my mobile is next to the bed. Call if anything changes. It doesn't matter what time.'

'Thanks, Zara, we really appreciate it.'

'No problem – and don't worry, it might be a false alarm.'

Mum's voice is cheery, but Mia can see from her frown that the young mare could be in trouble.

'That's a lot of money for one horse,' Mia says as her mother hangs up. 'Is Raven really worth twenty-five thousand?'

Mum nods. 'She's a huge investment for them. With this changeable farming weather, they've staked the success of their brumby project on Raven.'

'What's their brumby project?'

'Each time Raven wins a campdraft competition, Jude is able to use the money to truck dozens of horses south to new homes – the lucky ones that can be saved from culling.'

'Will you go out to help her?'

'Not unless I have to. I don't like the look of this weather and I don't want to leave you alone. Let's hope Raven settles overnight.'

'The kids on the bus said that even if this does blow

into a cyclone, it won't reach the coast before Sunday. If Raven's in trouble you should go, Mum – twenty-five thousand is a lot of money!'

'I know. If it were anyone else, I'd ask them to find another vet, but Jude is so generous with her brumby rescue program.'

'You are too, giving all those wild horses free dental check-ups.'

'It's the least I can do if someone's prepared to save them.'

'I'll be fine if you go. Everything's ready if the storm builds, and we have enough sandbags now to open an equine beach resort!'

Mum laughs. 'That's true. Let's see what happens in the morning.'

Seven

||||||||||||||||||||||||||||||||||||||||||||||||||||||||||||||||||||||||||||

After all the fresh air and sandbagging, Mia falls into a deep sleep, despite the shaking tin panels on the roof. Then, for the first time in over a week, her nightmare returns. A trapped dugong twists and shapeshifts, becoming net-tangled hatchlings. Then an adult turtle opens its beak to swallow a jellyfish. Mia sees that it's a drifting plastic bag.

'No!' she screams.

Mia wakes up trembling, but the ferocity of wind roaring around the house makes her quickly forget the nightmare. Maybe this *will* blow into a cyclone. She breath-counts the way the counsellor taught her, focusing on the memory of Bandit's soft muzzle, but then she thinks about that cephalopod incident. Did she imagine Erin smirking? Why would the older girl be so mean to her?

At last she drifts back into sleep.

Without the screech of corella alarm clocks, Mia wakes late. She checks the time, then rests for a moment, listening to water spilling over their gutters like wet season waterfalls.

'Morning,' Mum calls. 'The storm has been upgraded to a cyclone.'

'I'm not surprised. That wind's crazy!' Mia wanders out to the kitchen. 'What's this one called?'

'Cyclone Veronica. She's only a Category One, but they've issued an alert; just Blue for now, so it's still a school day.'

Mia groans. Blue is the lowest alert, warning that a cyclone *might* affect the area within forty-eight hours. 'That means our persuasive speeches will go ahead!'

'Unless they upgrade to Yellow before lunch.'

Yellow Alert means a cyclone is *likely* within twelve hours and they should start preparing. Mia pours muesli into a bowl and checks her weather app.

'Hmm, that's not likely,' she tells Mum. 'The cyclone is north of Broome, tracking slowly along the coast. It still might be a fizzer.'

Her phone rings. It's her dad.

'Hey, cara mia, are you all right? What's happening with that cyclone?'

'We're fine. Veronica is only a Category One. There's rain and howling wind, but so far, it's all good. This one is nowhere near as scary as Christine was.'

'Okay, that's a relief. We lost so many trees when she hit.'

Mia remembers her father's arms holding her safe through the worst of Cyclone Christine. She was only five in late 2013 when Christine ripped through

Wickham, uprooting gums and flinging branches around the garden of their old home. She shivers. By the following wet season her parents had split up. Then Mum sold the Wickham house and they moved out of town. That all seems like forever ago.

'How are things in Perth?' Mia asks.

'Good, everyone's fine.'

A sudden gust flings small branches onto the kitchen window.

'I'd better finish breakfast and sit with the rescue animals,' Mia says as the lights flicker. 'They hate this wind.'

'Okay, stay safe and keep in touch.'

'Thanks, Dad, I will.'

Mia stirs yoghurt into her muesli and rereads her speech. After breakfast Mum calls Jude to see how the young mare is doing. She turns the phone volume up to high so she can hear over the rattling windows.

'Raven had a bad night.' Jude's voice crackles on the speaker phone. 'She was pacing, then lying down, then pacing. And there seems to be some waxing around her nipples.'

'Okay, it sounds like you're right to be worried. She's definitely getting ready to foal. Or miscarry.'

'I'd rather be wrong,' Jude replies. 'If Raven wasn't the key to our brumby rescue program, I wouldn't dream of asking you to come out in this weather.'

'I know . . .'

Mia can see that Mum is torn. The wind is building and water will be gathering on the roads, but she loves what Jude is doing to help the wild horses. If this young mare dies, or has an internal injury and can't compete in campdrafts, Jude's brumby program will end.

'Let me check the latest cyclone update and I'll call you back in an hour.'

'Okay, thanks, Zara.'

'Are you going to go?' Mia asks between spoonfuls of muesli.

'Veronica is really slow moving.' Mum hesitates. 'She might track further down the coast or blow back out to sea, but I don't want to leave you alone when a cyclone is around, not even a slow-moving one!'

'If Veronica does cross land, the bureau says that's not expected before Sunday, still four days away.'

'Hmm.'

'You should go.' Mia understands why her mother is hesitating, but wants her to help rescued horses. 'I'll be all right here. You know I can look after everything.'

Mum paces the kitchen, then stares out the window into the rain. 'I hate leaving you.'

'I'll be okay. Everything is organised and you said yourself, Veronica is slow moving.'

'I know you can look after the animals, but . . .'

'Mum, go! You can't let Jude lose a horse worth *twenty-five thousand dollars*. Raven needs you and so do all those brumbies.'

'If I *do* go and can't get back till morning, you could stay at Kirra's place tonight.'

'As if I'd leave the animals on their own! We've been

through far worse than this, and Jimmy's at the end of the track if I need anything. Besides, you'll probably be home this evening.'

'You are so stubborn.'

'Where could I have got that from?'

They both laugh.

'Okay,' Mum decides. 'I'll drive out to Spinifex Downs after you're on the bus. In fine weather it's only an hour and a half away, but if there's water over the road, it might take longer. I'll check Raven and hopefully things will move along quickly with the foal. Then I'll be back tonight, or tomorrow at worst.'

Mia smiles, feeling proud that Mum trusts her to care for their menagerie on her own.

'I'll call Kirra's dad now and ask if he can give you a lift home after school, if I'm delayed.'

'What about Roxy?' Mia asks. 'Will you take her with you?'

'It's probably better if Roxy goes to school with you today. You know what foaling is like. I might not be able to manage regular joey feeds as well.'

'Roxy would be a perfect excuse for me not to do my speech.'

'Don't you dare,' Mum says, laughing. 'You know it's good to face your fears.'

There's an awkward silence as Mia bites her lip and looks at the floor, knowing they're both thinking about her panic attacks.

'With animals and cyclones, yes,' Mia says, lightening the mood, 'with public speaking, no.'

Mum hugs her. 'Your speech is a call to arms for the environment.'

'I guess so . . .'

Mum double-checks her mobile vet kit, while Mia pours Roxy's formula into bottles. They feed the possum and Mia runs out to fill the horse troughs.

'Stay dry,' Mia tells Bandit, Freckles and Sultan, 'and I'll see you after school.'

As they wait at the end of the track, Mum listens to Mia's speech.

'The beginning is great. I love the way you get straight to the point saying that we need to act to help fight climate change, then build the argument, but perhaps you could speak more slowly. You're still under the time limit, so there's no rush.' Bus headlights cut through the rain, and Mum asks, 'Are you sure you'll be okay?'

'Yes!' Mia pushes away her worries. 'We can't change our plans every time there's a cyclone off the coast.'

'Hey, I'm meant to be the adult here!' Mum kisses Mia's cheek and tucks the rug over Roxy. 'Stay safe. I'll be back as soon as I can.'

Mia waves as Mum's van disappears into the mist.

Shazza drives the bus slowly, listening to continual weather updates on the radio. All the little kids want to sit near Mia so they can look at Roxy. Jess and Kirra are just as besotted with the tiny pinkie, especially Kirra. Although her friends have both French-braided their hair like Erin's, there's no earphone-sharing today, and Mia is secretly pleased.

Halfway to Karratha, Mia hears a ping from the seat behind.

'They've upgraded Veronica to a Cat Two,' Nick tells her, checking his phone.

A moment later, Shazza taps the microphone she rarely uses.

'Listen up, guys, the cyclone's been upgraded . . .'

'Awesome.'

'Let's go home!'

'Hey, settle down,' Shazza growls. 'No one's going home! Now listen, even though it's now a Category Two, we're still on Blue Alert, so school is open and that's where I'm taking you until I hear otherwise.' The microphone squeals, interrupting her momentarily, then she adds, 'Stop moaning! Cyclone Veronica is heading southwards, so all you little geographers will know that Karratha is a safer place to be than at your homes in Wickham and Point Samson.'

They groan, but Mia sees the sense in Shazza's logic.

At school, their morning lessons drag. Double English class is after lunch and during the break Mia paces the undercover area, trying to manage her nerves.

'You'll be fine,' Jess says. 'Public speaking is good practice for someone planning to build a veterinarian empire.'

'I'm not planning a—'

'Or for working up an equine bling sales pitch,' Jess continues. 'Honestly, Mia, your sea-glass bridles are amazing. I've never seen anything like them.'

'There are bridles for sale online with crystal decorations,' Mia replies, 'but none with glass.'

'Recycling sea-glass is way better than fake crystal!'

Mia grins, and as they share a bunch of grapes from Kirra's lunch box, she dismisses the left-out feelings she's been having. Her friends are the best – she's been worrying about nothing!

The end-of-lunch siren sounds and Mia shudders.

Jess punches the air. 'Here we go!'

They get through the first fourteen speeches. Kirra talks about battery hens, and Jess nails her argument on the gender pay gap in sport. Some of the other kids seem nervous too, so that makes Mia feel better.

Jack is concluding his speech about protecting petroglyph rock carvings on the Burrup Peninsula when the siren sounds. Their teacher glares at anyone starting to pack up.

'Wait, please.'

'And to conclude,' Jack says, 'we are lucky to live by the site of the most abundant rock carvings in the world. Each image tells a story and I believe that business should not determine which rock stories remain. If we allow mining companies to destroy images, including those of the now-extinct Tasmanian tigers, we lose our shared culture. Thank you.'

They all give Jack a solid round of applause and begin packing up.

'Those who weren't able to present today can do so tomorrow,' Ms Malouf says. 'Depending, of course, on what our friend Cyclone Veronica does.'

Mia breathes a sigh of relief, then frowns, wishing her speech was over and done with. Like Veronica, it will be hanging over her for at least another day – or maybe more!

Her friends help with Roxy's afternoon feed, and before the end-of-school siren they hear that the cyclone's been upgraded to a Category Three: *risk of injuries and major property damage.*

'Don't worry,' the teacher on bus duty tells them, 'Veronica is still a long way off the coast.'

Shazza has replaced her normal mud mat with a heavy-duty model, and she's laid old towels along the bus aisle for extra protection.

'Wipe your feet carefully,' she orders as they step aboard. 'No one's slipping over on my watch.'

Ominous storm clouds threaten as they pass the Cossack turn-off. Kirra peers out the window. 'I guess we won't be seeing the Staircase to the Moon tomorrow night.'

'Not in this rain.' Mia rubs mist off the glass. 'And the next one isn't until April.'

Watching the full moon's reflection as it rises across the mudflats is magical, but the stair-like apparition only happens a few evenings each year. On clear Staircase nights, they love taking a picnic to moon-view at the old pearling port of Cossack.

'We could invite Erin to watch the next one with us,' Jess suggests.

'Sure.' Mia tries to make sense of the sinking feeling she gets whenever Erin's name is mentioned.

'She said her family would only be here for a few months, though.'

Shazza pulls up at the Wickam turn-off where Kirra's dad is waiting at the bus stop to drive Mia home. They listen to a weather update on the way.

Western Australia's north-west coast is bracing for widespread destruction as Cyclone Veronica slowly approaches. Veronica is expected to continue to strengthen to a severe category tropical cyclone, with a coastal crossing possible for the Pilbara next weekend. While no impact is expected for the WA mainland during the next forty-eight hours, communities along the Pilbara coast should begin preparing for what could be a dangerous period over the weekend. The passage of this intense and slow-moving system may lead to significant storm surge, prolonged wind and flooding.

'Are you sure you're going to be okay tonight, Mia?' Kirra's dad looks worried.

Mia slings Roxy's pouch over one shoulder. 'Mum will probably be back this evening, and a crossing is still days away. If she can't get home, I'll call if I need anything.'

'Make sure you do!' He hands her a bag with a container of food in it. 'That's some wattleseed shortbread and lasagne from the missus. She doesn't want you going hungry.'

'Thank you.' Mia laughs. 'I'll add it to the feast Mum left in the fridge.'

Eight

Mia bends to receive Biff's slobbery kiss, then waves as Kirra and her dad drive up the track. From their veranda, the stormy sky looks even more ominous than when they left school. Mia hangs Roxy's pouch over a chair in the lounge room, then races across to the stable. She's soaked by the time she gets there.

'Hello,' Mia calls, trying to keep her voice steady as the wind flicks branches against the roof. The horses are tossing their heads. They've been cooped up in the home paddock since morning. She opens the gate to the larger bush paddock so they can have a run, even though it means they'll need a rub-down later. Wet horses chill quickly. 'Have fun,' Mia calls as they canter into the pouring rain.

The teenage wallabies are next. They're mostly independent, but in weather like this, they get sooky and hang around the yard. Mia cuts carrots and gives them each a crunchy treat. The youngest teen hops into the kitchen and settles down beside Roxy's sling-pouch.

'Okay,' Mia tells the wallaby, 'I guess you can stay in tonight.'

She likes being home on her own, though she's never really alone, not with so many animals around. Mia gives Biff a bone from the fridge, then cleans the rescue possum's cage. She gives it a chunk of cucumber, grateful they released an injury-recovered microbat last week. That bat was a handful!

Mia turns on her laptop to check her new favourite site. It's an interactive map encouraging citizen scientists across Australia to report unusual marine life. She's logged two fish since getting involved. With warming seawater and more creatures drifting into new territories, Mia hopes the sightings will help researchers track what's going on and protect endangered species.

Before dark, she clangs the horses' chaff bucket and calls them in for their feed. They canter across the wet paddock, little Freckles leading the way. Mia rubs them dry then goes inside, cuts a huge slice of the chicken pie her mum left, and flops in front of the TV.

Her phone buzzes. It's Mum.

'Hi, Mia, how is everything?'

'The rescue animals are fed. The horses had a run and are back in the stable. It's windy but we're snug. How about you?'

'Jude was a bit overcautious calling me out, but I'm hoping Raven's labour will start soon. Now that I'm here, she wants me to stay and see it through, but if you're nervous being there alone, she says she'll manage without me . . .'

'Don't worry,' Mia reassures her, even though Cyclone Veronica's growling voice is beginning to make her uneasy. 'We're all fine.'

'Well, Jude will be relieved to hear that. How did your speech go?'

'There was only time for half the class to present. I was next speaker when the siren sounded, so I'll be first tomorrow.'

'I should be back late afternoon or evening. What are you doing now?'

'Eating dinner and watching a movie.'

'That sounds fun. I'll leave you to it and get back to Raven. Call if you need me.'

'Okay, love you, Mum. I hope everything goes well with the foaling.'

'Thanks, love you too.'

Mia takes a bite of chicken pie and turns up the volume. Biff isn't usually allowed on the couch, but he's padding around the room nervously, so she grabs an old sheet and makes an exception.

'Don't tell Mum,' she whispers, stroking Biff's soft ears.

Being home alone is exciting, but a bit scary as well. Her mother is often called out in the evenings; staying overnight is less common. Mia feels a warm sense of responsibility being trusted with the care of their home and animals. She just wishes it wasn't during a cyclone.

After the movie Mia and Biff walk around the house, checking and double-checking everything is secure. When she's sure everything is safe, Mia takes a few deep breaths and climbs into bed, setting the alarm for two a.m. so she can feed the pinkie. Biff curls on the end of her doona, nuzzling at her feet. Her heart rate settles, and despite the intensifying wind she falls into a deep, dreamless sleep.

Dozing off again after Roxy's two o'clock feed is more difficult. The house feels spooky in the early hours, with things scratching and thudding onto the roof. Mia stares at the ceiling, wondering whether Mum has delivered the foal yet.

As strange shadows fly past the window, the same old worries fill her mind; overwhelming environmental threats and endangered species. She needs to do more to protect them before it's too late. Then her thoughts drift to Erin and French braids and cephalopods.

Stop, she tells herself.

Mia takes a deep breath, focusing on each inhalation then observing the feelings in her body. Worries always feel worse at two a.m. than in daylight, but the trick works. The next thing Mia knows, she's waking up to cracks of dawn light peeping through her curtains.

She stretches and gets dressed, then sprints through rain and wind gusts to begin the morning feeds. She gives each horse a huge armful of hay before mucking out the stable.

'Sorry, guys, but you have to stay in the home paddock until this afternoon.'

Her phone suddenly lights up with a message from Mum.

Raven is progressing. Hope to have a foal soon.

Mia replies with a row of crossed finger emojis, then continues shovelling manure.

'Cooee.'

Looking around, she sees Jimmy unhooking their gate. He drives his old ute into the yard and leans out the window.

'You going to school today, Dimples?'

'Yep, it's still a Blue Alert. School's only cancelled when we get to Yellow.'

'Want me to drive you to the end of the track?' He pushes his old hat further back onto his head. 'Your mum said she might be away overnight, and I reckon it's too wet to wade all the way to the bus stop.'

'Thanks, Jimmy, that'd be awesome. I'll call my friend's dad and say they don't need to drive out from Wickham to collect me. Would you like coffee? I'm almost finished here. We don't have to leave for another half-hour.'

'I never say no to a cuppa.' Jimmy chuckles.

'Do you want to go ahead and flick on the kettle? And there are crumpets on the bench. If you toast a few, I'll get Roxy's pouch ready for school.'

'Rightio.'

As they eat breakfast the dogs play tug-of-war with a scrap of rope.

'How's your garden surviving the downpour?' Mia asks.

'Not bad, but the frangipani tree misses our Elsie.'

'Hmm.' Mia doesn't know what to say.

It's been nearly a year since Jimmy's wife died.

Elsie was the kindest person Mia knew, and she had a special knack for growing plants in the red pindan soil.

After Elsie passed, Jimmy kept to himself for months. They took him meals, but his blue eyes lost their twinkle and Mia remembers how he seemed to be fading. Then Mum asked Jimmy to help them with the horses. He came every day, oiling saddles and cleaning out the stable. After a while that set him right. Or right enough to manage his sadness and carry on.

Mum reckons Jimmy is the perfect neighbour – someone ready to help in a heartbeat, but who gives you plenty of space otherwise. After Elsie died, Mum and Jimmy set up an ultra-high frequency radio between their houses. It's a 'line-of-sight' system between antennas to use during emergencies if there are no other services available. When Mia's home alone, knowing Jimmy is at the end of the track near his UHF transmitter gives her peace of mind.

'What do you think about this weather?' she asks. 'You were right about it becoming a cyclone. The latest report said Veronica is way out at sea, so she still might blow past.'

'Mm, maybe, but my old bones reckon we'll take a hit later this week. The birds and ants get organised well beforehand. They know what's what.'

Mia shivers, glad Mum will be with her this evening. She wouldn't want to be alone at the height of a cyclone, or be the one to have to decide when it's time to set the horses free.

'We'd better go,' she says, checking her watch and gathering her things.

She quickly writes *I'm grateful we have a kind neighbour* in her gratitude journal. Then they drive to the end of the track and wait at the bus stop.

'Jeez, it's coming down!' Jimmy chuckles and asks, 'D'you know where the word "cyclone" comes from?'

Mia shakes her head.

'The Greek word *Cyclops*.'

'Those one-eyed giants who eat people?'

'That's right.'

'Our teacher told us a story about a Cyclops. He was the son of Poseidon, the ocean god.'

'We might need an ocean god soon.' Jimmy watches water gathering beside the road. 'There'll be flooding if this rain keeps up.'

They see lights cutting through the rain.

'Here comes Shazza,' Mia says as the bus splashes towards them like a big orange duck.

'Will you need a lift after school?' Jimmy asks.

'I'll be right, thanks. Mum should be back by then, but if not, my friend's dad can drop me home.'

'Okey-doke, Dimples. Send a message later today on the UHF if you need anything.'

'Thanks, Jimmy, I will.'

She tucks Roxy's pouch under her coat and makes a dash for the bus. Mia steps carefully between sodden floor towels, holding the roof rail as she edges towards her seat in front of Nick.

'Still no car?' she asks.

'I have zero chance of driving this week,' he grumbles.

'What's the wind like at your place?'

'Same as here. How are your horses?'

'They're okay. The wind is spooking them, but they've been through worse.'

At the Wickham turn-off Mia moves across to let Kirra sit down.

'You're soaked!'

'Umm,' Kirra points to the window with her painted nails, 'it's raining outside in case you hadn't noticed.'

'Where's Jess?'

'Her parents said she could stay home.'

'Lucky!' Mia stares out at the mist, then re-reads her speech. For the first time ever, she's not sure what to say to her oldest friend.

There's a buzzing cyclone excitement in the bus with all the kids wondering whether Veronica will cross the coast, and if so, will it be near them? The slow-moving cyclone is still a long way out to sea, but she's now a Category Five, the highest rating. Some of the newer students look worried. Cat Five winds are destructive, but those born in the Pilbara know it's rare to get a direct hit. Most cyclones weaken, or go east to Hedland, or south to Onslow.

Flooding in the low-lying areas around them is often more dangerous than high winds. Two-metre-tall indicator signs on Pilbara roads show drivers water depth, but people misjudge water on the highways and get into trouble crossing dangerous creeks. Then volunteer services need to go out and rescue them.

Mia and Kirra check the school's daily noticeboard, then head along a quiet corridor to their lockers.

'Where is everyone?' Mia looks around.

'Home, like Jess.'

As they reach their English classroom, Kirra squeezes Mia's arm. 'Don't worry, you'll be great.'

Mia takes a deep breath, visualises Bandit's warm face and clutches her notes.

'Good morning, class,' Ms Malouf says. 'With so few people here today, I've decided to postpone the remaining persuasive talks until after the cyclone.' She smiles at Mia. 'And that will give you more time to practise.'

Mia sighs. Speaking to a smaller group would have been so much easier.

Most of the teachers give the students who've turned up free time to work on assignments – all except Mr Finch, their Maths teacher. He decides it's a great time to spring a revision test on them.

Mia doesn't mind – she likes Maths. But Kirra is worried she'll flunk the test.

'What if it counts towards our term mark?'

'It can't if only half the class take it.'

The rain continues. They're waiting for Kirra's dad after school when Mum calls.

'How did Raven go?' Mia asks. 'Has her foal survived? Are you home?'

'Whoa, slow down, darling, one question at a time.' Mum hesitates for a moment. 'Raven hasn't delivered yet. It's classic first foaling behaviour. She's distressed and not progressing. She should be saving energy for the actual birth, but she's confused and pacing.'

'So you're still there?'

'Yes, I'm worried about Raven.' Mum pauses. '*And* I'm worried about you.'

Mia takes a deep breath. 'Don't be,' she says. 'Jimmy drove me to the bus stop this morning and Kirra's dad is dropping me home. I'm okay and you know I'll make sure the animals are safe.'

'Thanks, Mia. I'm so proud of the way you look after them while I'm away. You'll make a great vet one day, if that's what you decide to do.'

Mia beams, wanting to believe her mum, but vets need confidence. She worries that anxiety will stand in her way. And she's worried about being home alone another night.

'How did your speech go?' Mum asks.

'Ms Malouf put them off until after the cyclone.'

'Oh, are you happy about that?'

'I guess so, but it'd be good to have it over and done with.'

'And was Roxy okay?'

'Everyone wanted to hold her, even the teachers. You'd think they'd never seen a baby wallaby before. I had to keep explaining that pinkies need peace and quiet.'

Mum laughs. 'She *is* pretty cute. If the cyclone keeps tracking down the coast you can both stay home tomorrow if you like.'

'Even if it's a Blue Alert?'

'Yep. I reckon one day off school won't hurt.'

'Staying home would be great,' Mia replies. 'We didn't

do much today because there were so many kids away.'
She doesn't mention the surprise Maths test in case
Mum changes her mind.

Kirra taps Mia's shoulder and points to her dad in
the five-minute pick-up zone.

'I've gotta go. Kirra's dad is here.'

'No worries, I'll call again later. Stay safe.'

Nine

The dark clouds rolling in from the west look like colossal bruises on the sky. As they drive home, parts of Highway One are already submerged, especially the area south of Roebourne.

Kirra's dad taps the steering wheel. 'If this keeps up, I reckon some of the low-lying communities will flood.'

After the turn-off, Mia sees something white flapping beside the road. They pull over. The girls grab a towel and race back to find a small corella.

'Looks like it's been hit by a car,' Kirra says.

'Maybe.' Mia drapes the towel over the bird. 'Or it could be struggling to fly in this weather.'

She carefully wraps it. The corella squawks for a moment, then quietens.

'Can we save it?' Kirra asks.

'We can try.'

Kirra's mum has a cat, so the bird will need to go home with Mia. Another creature to care for! Lucky Mum is letting her stay home from school tomorrow.

Mia opens a corner of the towel as they drive along the wet road and does a quick visual examination. The corella's chest is skinny. It's an old bird with no muscle tone. She doesn't like its chances.

At home they settle the bird in a box, all awkwardness between them gone as Mia makes up an electrolyte solution to feed the bird. As she guides the bird's beak into a container of fluid, Kirra asks, 'Will it be able to fly again?'

'I hope so.' Mia doesn't want to give her friend false hope, but there's no point upsetting Kirra yet. Perhaps the corella *will* live. Sometimes injured birds surprise her. 'We'll know by morning whether it survives the shock.' Mia dunks the corella's beak again, taking care not to cover its tiny breathing holes. 'I'll text and let you know.'

Kirra and Jess are also staying home tomorrow, so Mia's looking forward to a day of online chats and bingeing movies. As long as Veronica doesn't crash the internet.

'Looks like you're ready for anything,' Kirra's dad says, nodding to the sandbags. 'Are you sure you won't be nervous on your own for another night?'

'I'll be fine.' Mia pushes aside thoughts of the spooky two a.m. branches thrashing the roof. 'I'm sure Mum will call soon with an update on the foal.'

'Okay, we'll get going then. Call if you need anything.'

Mia starts the afternoon chores. Jimmy calls her on the UHF radio to make sure she's all right, then Mum calls at dusk.

'Raven's making progress at last,' she says. 'I'm hoping we'll have a foal very soon.'

'That's great.' Mia tells her about the new patient. 'Should I offer the corella some fruit?'

'You could try mashed banana, but for now fluids are the most important. Sounds like you've done everything I would have!'

They chat for a few minutes before Mum has to go. After making dinner for herself and the animals, Mia gets back to reading and texting her friends. Despite the wild wind, she sleeps well.

Mia wakes to a message from Kirra.

How's the corella?

She looks at her clock and texts.

Why are you awake at 7? We don't have to go to school today.

I was worried about our bird.

I'll check and text back.

Mia pads out to the laundry where she left the corella in a box overnight. She peers in, expecting the worst. To her surprise the bird is alive. Not looking great, but still breathing. Its blue-ringed eyes blink as Mia puts a dab of mashed banana near its beak. Then she takes a photo of it pecking to send to Kirra, along with some smiley emoji faces.

Corella made it through the night.

That's great.

It's good to be back on common animal ground with her friend.

She spreads Vegemite across her toast and wonders when Mum will call. Maybe she's sleeping after a long night with the horses. Mia turns on the radio for a weather update. Cyclone Veronica was downgraded overnight from intensity Five to Four; instead of *potentially widespread destruction* the risk has now reduced to *significant roofing and structural damage and dangerous debris*.

Then the radio announcer advises:

Veronica is tracking slowly along the coast, more than 350 kilometres north-west of Port Hedland, and not expected to make landfall until Sunday morning. Communities along the coast remain on Blue Alert.

'Looks like we're safe for now,' Mia tells Biff. The kelpie licks her hand.

Mia hums to her music as she feeds the animals. She's cleaning their bedding when she hears a voice.

'Morning, anyone home?'

'Hi, Jimmy, come in.'

He leaves his muddy boots by the door and asks Mia if she needs a lift to school.

'All good today – Mum said I don't have to go to school.'

'Bonzer. Is there anything else you need?'

'No, thanks, I'm fine.'

Jimmy looks a little disappointed, so Mia quickly adds, 'The horses would love some company though. They're going stir-crazy in the home paddock. I was about to muck out their pens. If you have time, I'd love a hand.'

'Rightio.' He pulls on his boots and heads into the rain. 'I'm onto it.'

Mia brews coffee for Jimmy and makes herself hot chocolate. She covers the mugs with a small waxy-wrap to keep them warm and carries them to the stable where the old stockman is hard at work. They lay fresh straw, then sip companionably. Jimmy checks the runoff in the channels that Mia dug. 'That's flowing smoothly. Well done.'

She smiles at his praise, and while Jimmy checks the horses' hooves, Mia plaits Freckles's mane. Bandit snorts and tosses his head when she tries to comb his.

'If it gets much worse, you'll have to set them free,' Jimmy says.

'I know.'

Mum has taught her that it's safest for horses to be free during a cyclone, but knowing when to release them is tricky. Mia hopes against hope that the cyclone continues to be downgraded. She doesn't want to have to make that decision without Mum.

'We have another rescue patient,' Mia tells Jimmy, changing the subject.

'Stone the crows, what is it this time?'

'Not a crow, but close – it's a bird. Come and I'll show you.'

They return to the house and Mia carries the corella's box to the veranda. Jimmy holds the old bird steady in his age-spotted hands while she dips its beak into more electrolyte solution.

'The corella was too stressed to eat last night,' Mia tells him, 'but this morning it pecked some banana.'

'That's a good sign. Maybe with a bit of rest it will mend.'

Neither of them looks totally convinced.

After Jimmy leaves, Mia feeds the other animals then settles down with a book, trying to take her mind off the cyclone. Despite the weather update, it still feels like Veronica is strengthening. Her phone buzzes and Jude's name crosses the screen.

'Hi, Mia, your mum asked me to give you a quick call. Raven has foaled, but Zara needed to help her. The good news is that mare and foal both survived, but there's also worrying news. The foal is very weak.'

'Can Mum save it?'

'We're not sure. Zara is with them now. She wanted me to ring and make sure you're all right.'

'Please tell her that all our animals are safe, and Jimmy helped me muck out the stables this morning. He's just left.'

'Thank goodness you're okay.' Jude breathes a sigh of relief. 'I'm so grateful for your mum's help. If she wasn't here, both animals would have died last night. Raven is doing fine now, but Zara's barely left the foal's side.'

'I'm glad Mum could get out to you in this weather.'

'Me too. Thanks for being such a trooper, Mia. You're just like your mum – our horses are lucky to have another generation of safe hands into the future.' Mia doesn't know what to say, and is almost glad when Jude

adds, 'You've probably heard that the bureau is predict-
ing heavy flooding . . .'

'Mm, they've downgraded Veronica, but water is
already over the highway near Roebourne.'

'It's gathering here too. If the road south floods, our
neighbour can take Zara home in the chopper as soon
as the wind drops. Then, when the roads are clear, we'll
drive her van back.'

Mia isn't surprised. Most of the large stations use
helicopters for mustering. It's not unusual for Mum to
be collected by chopper in an emergency. Jude and her
partner don't own a helicopter, but neighbours in the
Pilbara help each other out.

'When you get a chance,' Jude adds, 'maybe you
could check that your helipad is clear?'

'Sure.'

'But only if it's safe to go outside. Just check for big
things. You can clear small branches at the last minute.
Once our foal is out of danger, your mum says she'll
call you.'

'No worries,' Mia says. 'I hope she can save the foal.'

'Me too.'

As Jude hangs up, Mia's phone pings. It's Kirra.

How's the bird?

Still alive. What are you doing?

Nothing much, let's group chat with Jess.

They FaceTime for a while, then send messages back
and forth until Mia's wi-fi goes down. She recharges her
phone, wondering whether her friends still have reception. Wickham has better range than their property.

Mia thinks about Erin and how keen her friends were to impress the new girl. If Jess and Kirra are online chatting without her, what are they saying?

She remembers the image she drew in her gratitude journal, of texting with her friends, and tries to think the best.

Biff drops his ball onto her lap. Mia rolls it across the room towards Mum's old surgery and he bounds back and forth happily. Then she listens to a new playlist and works on her jewellery, using pliers to attach sea-glass pieces to standard earring bases. If she's going to be an animal surgeon like Mum, she needs dexterity. Jewellery making is good practice. Mia wonders whether to decorate Bandit's halter with sea-glass. Maybe not, it could spook him, but Freckles might like some bling on her bridle.

All morning, needle-sharp rain pelts down, but the air is warm and muggy. It's an odd combination. Mia paces the house, glad not to be at school, but wondering what else to do. She checks the wi-fi. It's still down.

After lunch her phone pings with a short message from Mum.

Did Jude tell you Raven has foaled? She was too exhausted to push, but with help she got there. Now it's her colt that we're worried about.

Will he be alright?

It's touch and go. I'll call soon with more news.

I hope he makes it.

Mia makes a snack and reads her book, worrying about Mum and the foal. At last Mum calls back.

'How's the foal?'

'He's tiny and too weak to stand.' Mum sounds tired but determined. 'But I've given him a bag of plasma, and we're trying to milk Raven. Her little one needs colostrum as soon as possible.'

Mia knows the first twenty-four hours, when the mum's milk is rich with goodness, is a crucial time for a foal.

'Jude and I are taking turns to massage Raven's udders,' Mum continues, 'but she's skittish and won't let her foal near. You know how young mares are sometimes frightened of their babies . . .'

'Especially after a long labour.'

'That's right. Anyway, how are things there?'

'All okay.'

'Thank goodness. I'll call again soon.'

Mia turns on the radio, knowing that the ABC will have Bureau of Meteorology updates every fifteen minutes. After talking about Cyclone Trevor threatening the Northern Territory, the radio presenter switches to Western Australian weather warnings.

Cyclone Veronica remains a Category Four system which is moving slowly towards the Pilbara coast. An alert has been issued for communities between Pardoo and Mardie. All travellers are advised to leave the area and residents should enact their cyclone planning.

Mia checks a map on the wall. Pardoo is one hundred and thirty kilometres north of Port Hedland, and Mardie is a similar distance south of Karratha. Their home is right in the middle. What if the cyclone *does* hit while Mum's away? Mum's taken the van. She's stuck here for the duration. Mia chews her lip as the announcer continues.

People in the warning zone are likely to begin feeling the effects of this large cyclone overnight, with gale force winds developing. A severe coastal impact is expected over the weekend with destructive winds, very dangerous storm surges and heavy rainfall leading to major flooding. Evacuation centres are being set up in Karratha and Port Hedland ...

It's getting serious. Mia stands by the kitchen window, watching branches whip the air like brittle riding crops.

'Be strong, little foal,' she mutters. 'I need Mum to come home before this gets worse.'

Ten

||||||||||||||||||||||||||||||||||||||||||||||||||||||||||||||||||||||||||||||

Their emergency cyclone plan is pinned to the wall. Mia takes it down and begins working through the checklist, putting things she might need on the kitchen bench so they're easy to grab if the power goes out.

They have two big waterproof torches, a battery radio with plenty of spare batteries, towels and food for the animals as well as a first-aid kit. There are also backup medicines in Mum's office down by the gate. Some of them have to be kept in the fridge. Maybe she should run down and bring them to the house.

This reminds Mia that she needs to check the generator. It's in a small shed off the back veranda, and it should be fuelled up, ready to go if they lose power. She pulls on her coat and races to the shed. The generator splutters and burbles. Mia tries again, bending against the lashing rain. How does Mum do this so easily? She digs in her heels and pulls the cord. There's another splutter, then the engine roars into life. There's plenty of fuel. She turns it off, thankful but hoping she won't need it.

While she's outside, Mia runs down to collect Mum's vet medicine. She steps over the sandbags, checking none have shifted, and takes the supplies back to the home fridge.

'What else?' She dries her wet face, then remembers. 'Hmm, food for me.'

They always keep plenty of dried fruit and nuts. Mia adds a few containers to the pile on the bench along with bananas, crackers and a can of baked beans. Then she rechecks the emergency list. The most important thing is water. When there's flooding, sewage or chemicals can contaminate the mains, making it undrinkable.

She needs three litres per person or large animal for four days. Mia has never known a cyclone to last four days, but she follows the guidelines just in case, filling plenty of containers for herself and all the rescue animals. She even fills the bathtub with cold water. The possum watches her with big, wide eyes.

Her final job is taping the windows. The last thing they need is broken glass flying around the house. Mia unrolls strips of duct tape and places a big X shape across each of the glass panes. If the wind picks up and the panes buckle inwards, the X should hold them in place.

During the afternoon the wind strengthens. Between gusts, Mia runs out to check the helipad. She moves a few small branches, but otherwise it looks good. Mia knows the chopper pilot bringing Mum home will swoop over their house before landing, to let her know they've arrived. That'll give Mia time to check the pad again.

When everything's organised, Mia takes another

photo of the corella, ready to send to Kirra. The bird looks weak but it's still breathing. She feeds Roxy, tidies the kitchen, then wanders around the house, unsure what to do next. A pamphlet about Jude's brumby rescue program is on Mum's desk. She re-reads it, hoping the foal will pull through.

It's strange to be human-alone for this long. Mia begins practising her speech again, but the rattling windows unnerve her. She wonders how the horses are doing.

'C'mon, Biff, I'll race you to the stable.'

The kelpie isn't keen to go outside but he follows her into the storm. Mia strokes the horses. The shuddering stable roof is making them restless. They toss their manes and move away from her, stamping their hooves when Mia tries to soothe them.

Mia remembers Mum's words about setting the horses free before a cyclone hits. It's safer for horses to trust their instincts and find their own shelter, even though that feels weird for their human owners.

As the wind howls, Freckles snorts and Bandit pushes Mia's arm. Is it time?

She piles hay next to their feed trays and runs back to the house, wishing she could ask Mum. She tries to call her, but the phone rings out. A few minutes later, Mum calls back.

'Hi, Mia, the foal is stable for now. Is everything okay there?'

'I think so. I've checked the emergency kit and taped the windows.' Mia decides not to worry Mum with the latest cyclone update. 'If the wind strengthens, we're ready.'

'Well done.'

'But I don't know whether it's time to set the horses free . . .' Mia tells Mum about their fidgeting.

'They should be okay for a little while longer,' Mum replies. 'Veronica is still well off the coast, but if she *does* speed up and make landfall before I'm back, you'll know when it's time.'

'How?' Fear makes Mia's voice impatient. 'What are the signs?'

'Trust your instincts. It's hard to explain. They'll be pacing and edgy.'

'Mmhmm . . .'

That's what they're doing now, she thinks as Mum continues.

'It'll feel strange freeing them, but the horses will stick together and find somewhere safe to wait it out. Their biggest danger will be flying obstacles.'

'I know, Mum.'

'And when they return, they'll be chilled and hungry. You'll need to feed them as quickly as possible. Make sure there's plenty of hay and give them as much food as they can eat.'

'I have a pile of hay ready.'

Mum laughs. 'Of course you do.' Mia can hear the smile in her voice. 'Well, it sounds like you have everything under control. The mobile range in Jude's stable is hopeless, so if you call and I don't answer straight away, don't worry.'

'Okay, I'll leave a message if I need anything.'

'And then I'll reply as soon as I can.'

'Don't stress.' Mia tries to keep her voice light despite her anxiety. 'Everything's good here!'

'Thanks for being my backup, Mia. You're a champion. Now, I'd better get back to the foal. You sure you're okay?'

'Yes,' Mia answers confidently, even though she can feel her palms getting sweaty.

'Okay, that's great. I'm going to set up a sling for the colt to support his weight and then we'll try to get him to feed.'

'What colour is he?'

'Dark bay with a lovely white star on his forehead. Jude has named him Arrow.'

'He sounds beautiful. Take a photo if you have time.'

'Okay, I'll send one through when I can.'

'Thanks, Mum, I'm glad you were able to save them.'

'Me too, love you.'

After Mia hangs up, an image comes through on her phone. The photo shows Mum sitting beside a tiny foal lying on straw. Mia sends back a love heart, saves the image as her mobile's wallpaper and whispers, 'You can do it, Arrow.'

Then she turns back to the creaking, home-alone house, pushes away her fear and checks for messages from her friends.

There aren't any, but the wi-fi is back on! Jess has just posted on social media, so she must be connected.

Mia wonders whether to add a comment or wait until they contact her.

Meanwhile, Veronica continues spinning closer to land.

After feeding the wallabies and possum, Mia makes lasagne, eats some, then sets aside the leftovers. If their power goes down on the weekend, having cold lasagne will be better than crackers.

Mum sends a text.

Little Arrow is fighting for his life. Most foals would have given up hours ago. He's a battler.

Mia sends a thumbs up and turns on the radio. The Bureau of Meteorology is forecasting strengthening winds.

Around 7.30 p.m., a Yellow Alert is issued: *prepare for the arrival of a cyclone and get ready to shelter.* Mia keeps herself busy settling the animals for the night. What if the cyclone *does* hit before Mum gets back?

She paces the room. The thought of facing a cyclone alone makes her belly clench. Mia closes her eyes and takes ten deep breaths. Then she rechecks the emergency gear. Keeping calm is the most important thing she can do. The animals need her.

Knowing she can stay up as late as she likes feels odd, but good. Mia sends messages to her friends. Reception is patchy and their replies seem rushed and kind of distant. Maybe they're busy with cyclone prep and she's imagining it.

She takes a dab of banana mash to the old corella, then settles on the couch with a bowl of popcorn to watch a movie. Biff stares at her with pleading eyes and Mia lets him jump up beside her, glad to feel the snuggle of his comforting warmth.

A few hours later Mum calls again.

'Hope I didn't wake you.'

'No.' Mia laughs. 'Not with this wind tearing around the house! How's Arrow?'

'I reckon he's through the worst of it. We managed to milk Raven, and now Arrow is licking the bottle but not sucking. Jude squirted milk into his mouth so at least he's tasted some colostrum. We'll try again soon.'

'That's wonderful. When can you come home?'

'Hopefully at first light.'

'Great. How's Raven?'

'She's settled and letting her foal nuzzle, but Arrow's too weak to work out what to do. He's still in a sling to support his wobbly legs, but it shouldn't be long before he can stand on his own and suckle.'

'Jude must be so relieved.'

'She is, but enough of that. What's happening there?'

'Biff and I are watching old movies. The wind is yowling like feral cats, but our windows are holding. I'm glad I taped them.' Mia pauses. 'I can't wait till you're back, Mum. It's strange being here so long without you.'

'I wish I could jump in the car and drive home now, darling, but it's not safe with all this rain.'

'Is the highway south of Jude's place flooded?'

'I don't think it's too bad. We'll check in the morning, but Jude's neighbour said that if the water over the road is deep, she'll chopper me home as soon as it's safe enough to fly.'

'Cool!'

'If there's a break in the weather, try to check that our helipad is clear.'

'I went out earlier. It's fine for now.'

'Great. Don't panic if my mobile goes down, we'll swoop the house before landing.'

'Okay.'

'And in the meantime, Jimmy will be listening to the UHF channel if you need someone to talk to. I've gotta go, darling. I'm so proud of how brave you're being.'

'Thanks, Mum.'

Mia presses play on the remote control and strokes Biff's neck. They're snuggling together on the couch when he suddenly growls.

'What's wrong?' she asks.

Biff leaps off the couch, barking, and runs to the door. Mia follows. There are headlights at the gate. They're too high to be Jimmy's ute.

Her skin prickles. It's too late for visitors. She feels her heart race as a man's shape opens the gate. Mia peers into the squall as the car drives up to the house.

Eleven

||||||||||||||||||||||||||||||||||||||||||||||||||||||||||||||||||||||||||||

She holds Biff's collar as the man-shape opens the car door and runs onto their veranda. He steps into the light and relief floods through her. It's Nick.

'What's happened?' Her voice disappears into the wind.

'Dad's injured. We need your mum's help.'

'She's with a new foal.'

'Can you get her? Dad was fixing a mooring when another boat came loose and rammed him. He knocked his head and his arm is broken or dislocated or something. I don't know. It looks serious.'

'Mum's not here.'

'What?' He loosens his raincoat.

'She's helping a mare give birth at Spinifex Downs.'

'Where's that?'

'Halfway to Hedland.'

'Oh no.' Nick groans. 'She's the only person nearby with medical skills.' He rakes his fingers through his dripping hair. 'In this weather it could take an hour to get to Karratha. Could *you* help Dad? You often help your mum . . .'

'I don't know. I can try.'

'Dad's in the car.'

'Bring him in. Have you called triple zero?'

Nick shakes his head. 'The home line is down and my mobile's dead.'

'I'll call for the ambulance then take a look at his arm. We've just gone to Yellow Alert, but I think emergency services can still come out during Yellow. Is that right?'

Nick nods. 'Red is when you have to stay inside.'

While Mia calls triple zero from the veranda, Nick helps his father up the steps and into the house. Lorenzo is a strong, sun-bronzed fisherman, but tonight his face is pale with pain.

'Come and rest here,' Mia says, making space on the wide couch and putting a cushion under his elbow.

'Emergency services,' the switchboard operator answers. 'Do you need police, ambulance or fire services?'

'Ambulance.' Mia flicks her mobile onto speaker phone.

'Connecting you now . . .'

While she waits to be connected, she points to her phone charger in a power socket. Nick plugs in his phone.

Lorenzo bites his lip, trying not to moan as Mia's phone lights up.

'Please state the nature of your emergency,' another operator asks.

'My friend's father has crushed his arm. We're not

sure how badly it's broken, or if it is broken. My name is Mia and we live near Wickham.'

'Is the patient conscious?'

'Yes. He also banged his head. There's a lump on his forehead.'

'Please hold while I contact the nearest paramedics.'

'Okay.'

Mia puts her phone where reception is best, locks Biff in her bedroom to stop him licking everyone, then she wraps an icepack in soft cloth.

'Hold that on your dad's forehead.' She hands it to Nick.

Then Mia studies his bruised and swollen arm. The first responsibility of a medical worker, for animals or humans, is not to cause more harm. Mia wants to help, but she's worried about doing something that might worsen the situation.

'Have you had any pain relief, Mr Lombardi?'

'Please call me Lorenzo,' he groans.

'Only two Panadol,' Nick interrupts. 'I wanted to get Dad here as quickly as possible, while we could still cross the bridge. Luckily, we had Panadol in the glove box.'

'Hello?' Mia hears a voice and picks up her phone.

'I'm Kim from St John Ambulance Karratha. Is the patient able to speak to me?'

Mia holds the phone for Lorenzo, and he mumbles answers to Kim's questions.

Then Kim tells Mia, 'We need to get Mr Lombardi to hospital. I'm trying to contact Wickham medical services, but their lines appear to be down. We'll check with State Emergency Services and the nearest weather station to determine whether it's safe to send an ambulance out from Karratha.'

'Okay.'

Mia explains that Lorenzo is in a lot of pain but that his condition doesn't seem to be life-threatening.

'Our lines are very busy. I'll call back as soon as I can. Please stay near your phone.'

Mia offers Nick's mobile number as backup in case hers drops out.

'Wow, you're so practical in a crisis,' Nick says, 'like your mum.'

'I wish Mum *was* here,' she replies. 'She'd know how to treat your dad. All I can do is try to stabilise him.'

Lorenzo shifts his arm a little and gasps in pain.

'You're managing better than me,' Nick whispers. 'I'm worried that I might have hurt Dad's arm more, racing through the rain to get here.'

'Being stuck in Point Samson without medical help or reception would have been worse, especially with that lump on his head.'

'I guess so.' He squeezes her arm. 'Thanks.'

Mia feels her cheeks warm. 'While we wait for them to call back, how about I ring Mum and ask if we can give your dad some stronger pain relief?'

'That would be great.'

'And let's send a photo of his injuries. She might be able to tell us if we've immobilised his arm properly.'

'Brilliant!'

As Mia takes photos of Lorenzo's arm, Nick asks, 'Is there anything else I can do to help?'

'Maybe ease another cushion under his elbow, unless that's too painful for him. Then grab a doona from the bed and make sure he's warm.'

'The doona will get wet . . .'

'That doesn't matter – we have spares. When you've done that,' Mia adds, pressing Mum's speed dial link, 'fill the kettle and make him a hot drink. Small sips of milky tea with plenty of sugar is good for shock. Or ginger tea, if he likes that. There's some in the cupboard.' Then she turns to Lorenzo. 'Mr Lom . . . umm, Lorenzo, what would you say your pain rating is, between one and ten?'

He thinks for a moment, then says, 'Six.'

Mia knows Lorenzo is a strong, hardworking man. Six could easily mean someone else's eight or nine.

Mum's phone rings until her voicemail answers, 'Hello, this is Zara from Pilbara Animal Care. Please leave a message and I'll get back to you as soon as I can.'

'Mum, it's Mia. Can you please call? It's important.' Mia hangs up then tries again. 'Come on, Mum!' She taps her fingers on the table. There's still no answer. Mum must be out of range.

'There's also a gash on Dad's foot,' Nick tells her. 'I tied a bandage around it, but he was hobbling, so it's all muddy now.'

Mia gets antiseptic and a fresh bandage from their medical cupboard. She elevates Lorenzo's foot and adds an icepack.

'Is that okay?'

He grits his teeth, nods and closes his eyes.

'How long ago did you give your dad Panadol?'

Nick looks at his watch. 'About an hour.'

'Okay, we'd better hold off a little longer,' Mia replies. 'While we wait I'll check the wound and see what I can do. Mum has a pile of medical textbooks we could look through.'

She holds Lorenzo's foot and gently unwraps the bandage. The gash looks deep and there's a lot of blood.

Mia takes a deep breath, takes another photo to show Mum, then pours saline water over the wound.

'That's worse than I thought,' Nick says with a gulp.

'Mum's taught me how to stitch small wounds and to help horses foal, but I've never dealt with anything like this on my own.'

'Me neither,' Nick mutters.

They stare at each other.

Lorenzo opens his eyes and studies Mia's face as Nick holds the sweet tea to his father's dry lips.

'It's bad, no?' Lorenzo asks.

'As long as we can stop the bleeding it should be okay.'

Mia packs the wound with plenty of gauze and wraps Lorenzo's foot tightly, trying to decide what to do next. She checks her phone. No reply from Mum or the ambulance service.

'Is it okay if we raise your foot a little higher?'

'Si . . .'

They pack pillows and cushions under Lorenzo's

lower leg. Nick offers his dad more tea, but Lorenzo seems happier to drift in and out of sleep.

'We don't want him to lose consciousness,' Mia whispers. 'I'll look up head injuries, then try to work out what's happening with his arm.' She scans her mother's textbooks.

As she flips through the fracture and dislocation pages, Nick describes the drive from Point Samson. 'I'm used to cyclones and flooded roads,' he says, glancing over at his dad, 'but crossing that bridge did feel a bit risky.'

'How deep was the water?'

'Hard to know. Probably only a couple of centimetres over, thankfully, but flowing pretty fast.'

'Lucky you left when you did. It won't be safe for much longer.' Mia adds, 'It's kind of funny that your dad was worried about you driving to school when it was just a Blue Alert. And now you got to drive his new four-wheel drive in a full-on cyclone!'

'To be fair, it was an emergency. All I kept thinking about was getting him to you guys.'

Mia tingles at his words. 'You guys' means her as well as Mum.

'Does your mum know about the accident?' Mia asks.

Nick shakes his head. 'I didn't want to worry her. She can't do anything from Perth. Once Dad's settled, I'll call from Karratha. If we can get there . . .'

The phone rings. It's Kim from emergency services.

'Hello, Mia, we're going to send our first available ambulance from Karratha. It shouldn't be too long. Can you tell me exactly where your property is located?'

Mia gives clear directions and answers Kim's other medical questions as best she can.

'Thank you, we'll ring back when the paramedics are leaving the centre.'

Nick high-fives Mia, then shares the news with his dad. It's only a few minutes before Kim calls back.

'An ambulance has left Karratha to collect Lorenzo and transfer him to hospital. Depending on the weather, they'll be near Wickham in forty minutes. What's the condition of your track?'

Mia doesn't know, so she hands the phone to Nick.

'Hello,' he says. 'This is Lorenzo's son. The track is pretty rough, but I have a four-wheel drive. We could meet you at the Wickham turn-off.'

'Is your father well enough to travel in your car?'

Nick looks at Mia.

'I think so,' she replies.

'Okay,' Kim agrees. 'Just a moment – the Karratha team are saying they'll meet you at the pullover bay beside that big yellow mining truck. Does that make sense?'

'Yes.'

'If the roads are safe enough to return, the paramedics can then take Lorenzo and his son to Karratha Hospital in the ambulance.'

They wrap Lorenzo's wounded foot in plastic to keep it dry. There's still time for Mia to pour hot chocolate into a flask and cut a slab of fruitcake for the journey. Then they link arms to make a human sling seat for Lorenzo to sit on, and carry him out to the car.

Once he's settled on the back seat with the doona, Nick gives her a quick hug. 'We're so lucky you were here, Mia.'

'Thanks.' She looks at the floor, feeling suddenly shy. 'And don't worry. I'm sure your dad is going to be fine.'

'Thanks to you.'

'Drive carefully,' she calls, tightening her raincoat.

The car tail-lights disappear into the rain and Mia crosses her fingers, hoping that Nick and his dad will be okay. She huddles on the veranda for a moment, feeling horribly lonely.

'Breathe,' she tells herself. 'Everyone's okay.'

Then she hears the horses scream.

Twelve

||||||||||||||||||||||||||||||||||||||||||||||||||||||||||||||||||||||||||||||||

Mia sprints to the horse yard. Three misty shadows pace the fence-line. Branches thud against the stable roof and Freckles shrieks as a chaff bag flies across the yard. The pony's distress pushes Mia into action.

Her instincts are clear. It's time to free the horses.

Their big heads stretch over the fence, nostrils flaring, eyes wide. Mia remembers Mum's advice: *Setting horses free during a cyclone is the safest thing. They'll find their own shelter.*

She takes a deep breath and flings open the gate. The horses rear and scream and gallop into the mist.

'Be careful.' Mia's voice is shaky as she watches them disappear into the storm. 'Stay together. Be safe.'

She leaves plenty of dry food in the stable. When they return, Sultan, Bandit and Freckles will be desperate for feed, and their coats will be freezing.

Horses eat up to twenty-three hours a day, but that's not possible during a cyclone. Mia remembers Mum's instructions. *Wet horses need immediate care. Get*

112

plenty of warm blankets ready, and as much food as they can eat.

Leaving a mountain of hay for the horses makes her feel a little better. She's done everything she can.

Bang!

The stable door thuds against the wall. Mia hooks it onto a nail, ties open the main gate then darts back to the house. Debris is flying across the yard. She covers her head with her arms.

As Mia reaches the veranda there's an almighty crash. She turns. A branch has fallen onto the stable roof, crushing the place where she was standing a moment ago.

She pictures the horses' wide, panicked eyes as she freed them. Did Freckles sense this would happen? Mia's seen enough mysterious animal reactions to know it's possible.

Her pulse races. What if the horses had been inside? What if she'd stayed a moment longer filling their feed buckets? Sweat trickles down Mia's back as she stares at the stable. She leans against the front door, clenching her fists while the familiar fear of losing control spins through her mind.

Then she hears Biff. He's still in the laundry. His howl cuts through her fear. Mia digs her nails into her hands, taking three deep breaths. The animals need her. She can't panic now.

'I'm coming, Biff!' Mia shouts. She runs to the laundry and frees the kelpie.

Biff's nose goes into overdrive. He sniffs her arms

and legs, then circles the room, smelling the story of everything that happened while he was locked up.

'It's okay,' Mia whispers. He licks the rain from her face and nestles his nose against her. 'It's okay,' she repeats. 'I'm here, we're safe.'

Once her hands stop trembling, Mia packs away the antiseptic and gauze she used to treat Lorenzo. She wonders whether Nick has reached Wickham safely as she settles Biff and makes more hot chocolate. Then she flops onto the couch.

Mum calls as she's taking her first gulp.

'Darling, are you okay? I just got your message. What's happened?'

'It's all right, Mum. I'm fine and so are the animals.' Mia hears her mother's sigh of relief. 'I've set the horses free.'

'Oh Mia, well done – that must have been a tough decision.'

'As soon as I opened the gate they galloped into the storm. It was as if I wasn't even there!'

'You know horses shift into flight behaviour when they're terrified. They'll wait it out somewhere they feel safe.'

'I thought the stable would be the safest place, but . . .' Mia wonders whether to tell Mum about the crushed roof, or to wait till she's back.

'Don't worry,' Mum says. 'They'll trust their instincts.'

'But what if Freckles can't keep up with the bigger horses? She isn't a fast runner.'

'Freckles is canny and that's more important during

a cyclone. They'll stick together. The other two are probably already following her lead.'

Imagining that makes Mia smile.

'If they return before I'm back, don't forget to dry the horses quickly,' Mum says, 'otherwise they'll chill.'

'I know.'

'I'm so sorry I'm not home.'

'It's okay, but that's not everything,' Mia tells her. 'Nick's father was injured.'

'Oh no – is Lorenzo okay?'

'I think so. They came here looking for you. I did my best to help. Now he and Nick are meeting an ambulance at Wickham.'

'Goodness, what a night! Tell me everything from the beginning.'

Mia describes Lorenzo's injuries and explains how she raised his arm and wrapped his foot.

'Was that the right thing to do? I took photos to send, but I guess you were out of range, or maybe I didn't reduce them enough.'

'I didn't get them. Try sending the photos one at a time. Jude's internet keeps dropping in and out, so the fewer the better.'

Mia resends the images as they talk.

'Got them.' Mum's quiet for a moment, then says, 'You've done a terrific job, Mia. I'm so proud of you. I'll have to make use of your medical skills more often!'

'I was nervous,' Mia admits, 'and scared I'd do something wrong.'

'That's always how I feel when I assess new patients,' Mum replies.

'Really?'

'Mmhmm.'

'I didn't know that.' The wind howls as Mia thinks about Mum's words. Then she asks, 'So what's happening with Arrow? Is he okay?'

'He's stronger, but not out of the woods. He's drinking from the bottle at last, but the sling is still supporting his weight. If we get him standing in the next few hours, he might learn to suckle before I leave.'

'Then he can bond with Raven and grow stronger.'

'And Jude won't have to bottle-feed him.' Mum pauses. 'In the meantime he's keeping us busy. What's happening with your corella?'

'It's still alive.'

'Great.'

As they talk, Mia's phone pings. It's a text from Nick.

Got to the ambulance ok. On the way to Karratha. Thanks for everything. Talk tomorrow.

'I got a text from Nick,' she tells Mum. 'They met the ambulance.'

'Thank goodness,' Mum mutters. 'I wonder whether they'll transfer Lorenzo to Perth with the Royal Flying Doctor.'

'Would RFDS take Nick as well?'

'Maybe.'

Mia sends a row of smiley faces to Nick and feels her shoulders soften, picturing Lorenzo safe in the paramedics' care.

'Are you sure I did the right thing freeing the horses?

'Yes, I know it feels strange. Freeing them took courage, Mia.'

As Mum asks about the other animals, Mia's phone buzzes with a call. Dad's name flashes across the screen. Although her parents get on well, her father would be frantic if he knew Mia was home alone with a Category Four swirling near the coast. Mia lets the buzzing continue. She'll send him a text later.

'What time will you call in the morning?' Mia asks.

'As soon as we know the road condition. Have you heard the latest cyclone update?'

Mia checks the BOM site. 'We're still at Yellow Alert,' she says, 'and Veronica is tracking slowly. She's not expected to cross the coast until Sunday.'

'That's good. If I leave at first light, there'll be plenty of time to get back safely.'

'Okay,' Mia replies, although it feels as if the cyclone is building faster than the bureau's report. She shrugs. BoM's instruments and weather charts must know more than she does.

'Okay,' Mum says. 'I'll call to let you know when to expect me. It could be a slow trip home. There's mobile range about halfway, so keep your phone handy.'

Mia hears Jude calling in the background.

'I'd better go,' Mum says.

After hanging up, Mia sends a short text to her dad.

Hi Dad and Elena, sorry I missed your call. All okay here. I'm settling the animals and it's hard to talk over the wind. Can I call you back tomorrow?

Okay, little one, stay safe xxx

Dad loves emojis, so Mia replies with a string of hearts, kangaroo and horse images.

After so much excitement, Mia's sure that getting to sleep will be impossible. Adrenaline is racing through her body like a fizzing bath bomb.

Biff is crouching by the front door, so she lets him out to pee, laughing when he returns in record time.

'Shake on the mat,' Mia warns.

Biff does as he's told, and she gives him a doggy treat. He curls up by the bed while Mia feeds Roxy and checks the possum. Mia listens to a meditation app, but the gentle waterfall sounds are drowned by ferocious torrents of rain. She lies in bed, staring at shadows on the ceiling as rain hammers the roof. Counting sheep, or even sheepdogs, has never worked for her, so Mia thinks about how she treated Lorenzo. Could she have done anything better?

Mum often says that reviewing each operation is something vets do to improve their practice. Lorenzo isn't an animal, but he *is* her first solo patient. And more than anything Mia wants to be a good vet.

At last she drifts into sleep. When the alarm rings, it seems like she's only slept for a moment. Mia strokes Roxy's belly while the joey slurps her bottle, then she waits for Roxy to toilet. When that's done, Mia tucks the pinkie back into her flannelette pouch and falls into a deep sleep.

Images of birds flying through cyclonic winds and turtle hatchlings struggling to escape waterlogged burrows haunt her dreams. Mia shudders awake, then feels Biff licking her cheek.

'Ew, you have bone breath.' He licks her again. Mia sits up and ruffles the kelpie's ears. 'Was I yelling? It's okay, mate, just another nightmare.'

She shuffles to the kitchen, still half-asleep, and pours a glass of juice. It's almost seven, but the dark sky makes it seem like late afternoon. There's no message from Mum. Mia wonders how early she'll be able to get away from Spinifex Downs.

Time to feed the menagerie. She mashes banana and takes it to the corella. As she opens the box, Mia sees a frail little body lying motionless. The bird is cold. Mia's shoulders hunch. The corella was old and malnourished. Not every patient survives, she knows that, but telling Kirra will be hard. Mia loves wild creatures as much as her friend does, but Kirra's more sentimental.

Mia smooths the bird's feathers, then wraps it in an old tea towel. At least it died in a snug box. That's better than flailing about in this wind, or being attacked by eagles in a roadside puddle. She places the tea-towelled body into a plastic bag and puts it in the freezer. Once the rain stops, she'll bury the bird in the memorial corner of their garden. It will be in good company there.

Thirteen

||||||||||||||||||||||||||||||||||||||||||||||||||||||||||||||||||||||||||

Mum calls just before eight a.m.

'How far away are you?'

'Still at Jude's.'

'Oh.' Mia bites back her disappointment.

'Arrow collapsed soon after midnight. I'm not sure whether I can save him. His little belly was so swollen. I had to give him an enema to get his system working.' Mum pauses, sounding exhausted. 'There might be an internal problem. Jude and I are still milking Raven every two hours. How are you and the animals?'

'We're okay.'

'That's a relief. Once Arrow is stable, I'll take a power nap then get the van on the road. Hopefully in about an hour. If electricity goes down before I'm home, you'll need to start the generator. Do you remember how?'

'Turn on the fuel valve, check the choke, then press ignition. I know, I've already checked it!'

'Good. Let it warm up and then change the house switch to "generator", and don't forget to make sure the generator canopy is protected from rain, and *don't* bring it inside.'

'I know, carbon monoxide exhaust fumes . . .'

'And if I don't call again before I leave, it's because communications are down. Jude's stable has been through plenty of cyclones, without any problems, but her phone line is another matter.'

'All right.' Mia takes a deep breath.

'You're managing everything so well, darling.'

'Thanks, Mum. Don't forget to use your back-brace.'

Mia can feel a smile in her Mum's voice as she promises that she will.

'I love you. Stay inside as much as possible and keep safe.'

After hanging up, Mia battles her emotions. She tries to be understanding. Jude and the horses need Mum, but as the wind howls over the roof, Mia can think only one thing: *I need her too.*

The ten-thirty a.m. weather report makes her even more uneasy.

Communities along the Pilbara coast can expect conditions to deteriorate throughout Saturday with destructive winds, hazardous storm surge and heavy rainfall conducive to major flooding. Current tracking shows Veronica nearing the coast as a Category Four. Residents should prepare for wind gusts in excess of 125 kilometres. Landfall is likely Sunday morning between Port Hedland and Karratha with extreme winds up to 225 kilometres.

Mia shivers. Their property is just under fifty kilometres from Karratha and just over two hundred kilometres from Port Hedland. Mum and Jude are about midway. Tonight will be a sleepless night for them all, but at least Mum will be home soon.

Her mobile pings. It's from Nick.

Dad settled at Karratha Hospital. Arm badly crushed, but doc says he's going to be fine. Might be multiple fractures. Waiting for X-ray. Dad will fly to Perth with RFDS. Mum meeting him there.

Hope it's not multiples, Mia texts. Should we have treated it differently?

Nah, immobilising was the right thing. Is your mum home?

Still with the foal at Spinifex Downs.

You and the animals ok?

Mia hesitates. We're ok. You?

All good. Dad and I worried about you. Call us anytime.

Mia smiles.

Thx. I'm ok for now, the animals are keeping me busy! ☺ ☺

She re-reads her words and realises that she *is* okay. This brutal wind and rain will pass. Mum will be home soon. In the meantime, she has Biff to guard her and animals to protect. And if they smell her fear, the animals will become more jumpy.

'You've learned how to manage stress,' Mia says, raising her chin, 'so stop feeling sorry for yourself.'

The bossiness in her voice makes her laugh. She does some relaxation exercises then notices Biff trembling. Mia gives his back a gentle massage between stretches, then forces herself to focus on twisting wire around sea-glass.

Something crashes on the back veranda. Biff growls and Mia runs to the door. She eases it open and a guilty-looking wallaby stares at her. It's Dodger, one of the teenagers, and he's surrounded by accomplices. They've kicked in a screen and now they're huddling by the doorway, looking frightened and bedraggled from the storm.

'Oh, all right,' she mutters. 'Quick, hop inside!'

Mia herds the wallabies into the hallway and builds a barrier to the lounge room. She and Biff need at least one marsupial-free zone. Dodger settles down, looking very pleased with himself.

She peers outside to assess the damage. It takes all her strength, battling wild wind gusts, to drag the screen into place. Once it's secure, Mia tapes down the sides, using half a roll of packing tape.

When that's done, she feeds Roxy then cuts slices of apple for the teenage wallabies, trying to be stern with Dodger. His long-lashed eyes always melt her heart. Mia moves Roxy's pouch to the wallaby zone, rubs her aching shoulders, then checks the bathroom possum. Its wounds are healing nicely. She changes the newspaper at the bottom of its cage. The little ringtail is nocturnal, so it watches her with dazed brown-button eyes.

'Hey, sleepyhead,' she coos, 'I wonder whether we'll have you long enough to give you a name.'

The possum blinks and hides under the fresh newspaper.

Mia turns up the radio for a weather update, crunching a handful of almonds as she listens.

Cyclone Veronica continues moving slowly towards the Western Australian coast with Pilbara residents currently experiencing severe wind gusts . . .

As if on cue, branches slam onto their roof. Mia wishes Mum would hurry up and get home. If a metal sheet flies off she'll be in real trouble.

'You'd better survive, Arrow,' Mia mutters to the faraway foal, 'and make it worth delaying Mum for so long!'

The UHF radio crackles. Mia lifts the receiver.

'G'day.' Jimmy's voice sounds like it's coming from some faraway planet. 'You all okay? It looks like Veronica means business. Over.'

'Hi, Jimmy, it's Mia. Yes, our roof is holding so far, over.'

'Bonzer. Dog and I are snug as well . . .'

As Jimmy talks, a puddle forms around Mia's feet. She looks up at the ceiling, but there's no gap. Then she hears a sploshing sound. The wallabies have kicked over their water bucket.

'Sorry, Jimmy,' Mia says. 'The wallabies are inside and they're up to mischief. Can we talk later?'

'No worries. Stay safe and keep in touch, over.'

'Will do. You too.' She hesitates, then adds, 'Over.'

Mia cradles the receiver, then turns to Dodger and his gang. 'You guys are impossible! Don't you know fresh water is precious during a cyclone? This weather might go on for days.'

She covers the wet hallway in towels and the wallabies bounce over to nuzzle her hand.

'No more treats,' Mia tells them sternly. 'Our supplies need to last.'

They sniff the towels and try nibbling the soft fabric.

Mia refills their water bucket from the bathtub and weighs it down with a rock.

'Don't drink it all at once, or we'll be on rations.'

They click softly in reply.

As the cyclone builds, Mia works on her persuasive speech assignment, trying to take her mind off Mum and their horses out in the storm. She thinks about Erin's mean comments and the way Kirra and Jess seemed so desperate to impress the new girl.

When Jess became friends with her and Kirra, it was tricky at first, but soon three became better than two. It's worked for years, but things feel a bit different now. For a while, Jess and Kirra have been into things that don't really interest Mia, like make-up and talking about the boys at school. The guys are okay, but Mia doesn't want to change herself to try to impress them. Perhaps *she's* becoming the odd one out.

She jiggles her phone. What's wrong with her friends? Mia feels like sending them a capital letters text, reminding them that they're good as they are. They don't need to change. She stretches her hands. They're practical, like Mum's – nail polish would be totally wasted on her.

When she moves closer to the veranda, her phone pings. It's a text from Kirra. Mia's skin tingles. It's as if her friend read her mind.

How's the corella?

Mia doesn't want to share the bad news via a text message. She'd rather tell Kirra in person.

All good.

Mia sends photos of little Roxy and the cheeky wallabies as a distraction, then texts, How's the weather there?

Crazy!

There's no weather station at Wickham or Point Samson, so Mia has to rely on radio updates from other towns; Roebourne, Karratha or Port Hedland. Each station records different details, but all warn about the risks of flooding. Veronica's crossing will coincide with abnormally high tides. And because the cyclone is slow moving, the weather forecasters warn that dangerous volumes of water could quickly accumulate.

The midday news is even more frightening.

A severe flood watch is forecast for much of the Pilbara, with some areas set to receive between 100 and 500 milli-metres of rain; more than their annual rainfall in a few days ...

That's a lot of rain!

Mia sprints across the yard to Mum's surgery, checking there are no gaps between the sandbags. With so much rainfall, lower parts of their property will probably flood, but the sandbags are secure. She runs back, changes out of her dripping clothes and wonders what to make Mum for lunch.

Meanwhile, the teenage joeys hop along the hallway, sparring and jumping. Biff whimpers as Mia paces the room. *Where's Mum?*

She rings at last.

'Hello, darling, sorry it's taken so long to call back. Jude's power is down. I've had to recharge my phone via her generator.'

'Did Arrow pull through?'

'Yes! We were able to save him, and now he's feeding without help.'

'That's great news.'

'I'm watching him rest quietly with Raven, wishing *I* was home resting with my little one . . .' She pauses. 'Mia, I have some bad news.'

'What?' Mia digs her nails into her palms.

'The highway south of Spinifex Downs is flooded. It's too deep for me to drive through.'

Mia takes a deep breath. 'Are you sure?'

'Jude's been in contact with the SES. They say it's too risky. She's trying to call her neighbour about flying me back in the chopper, but they aren't answering. Jude thinks their line is down.'

'Oh.'

'That means I might not get home until after Veronica passes.'

Mia clutches Biff.

'Are you there?'

'Yes, Mum.'

'I'm so sorry, darling.'

Mia takes a deep breath, imagining her head resting against Bandit's neck, but that doesn't help. She can only picture torrential rain soaking his coat.

'I need you to be strong, Mia. If you call Jimmy via the UHF channel, I'm sure he'll come over . . .'

Mia looks out at their sodden track. The last thing she wants is for Jimmy to risk getting bogged in his old ute. His dodgy hips would never make it up the track. She steadies her shaking hands and takes another slow breath.

'It's okay, Mum. The roof and windows are holding and by this time tomorrow the cyclone will have crossed.' Her calm voice surprises her. *Maybe I'm stronger than I realise.*

'I promise I'll be home as soon as I can,' Mum says, 'and in the meantime, call me anytime, for whatever reason. My phone is charged and it's in my overalls pocket.' She pauses. 'I'm so proud of how resourceful you're being.'

'Thanks, Mum.'

After they hang up, Mia grits her teeth. 'I can do this.' She pushes away her fears to focus on practical things, makes a list and gets started.

Fourteen

||||||||||||||||||||||||||||||||||||||||||||||||||||||||||||||||||||||||||||||

By early afternoon, Mia has completed all the jobs on her list. She'd forgotten how loud the noise of a cyclone can be. Like a triple road train bearing down on her. She tries not to panic as the windowpanes bulge inwards.

Being home alone for so long is weird. Mia remembers Dad's arms holding her close during Cyclone Christine and wishes he were here now. Biff licks her hand, sensing her distress, and she hugs the kelpie to her chest.

When Dad calls again, Mia doesn't reply, but sends a message to reassure him that she's safe.

The wind is deafening. I can't hear very well, so let's text instead.

Okay, cara mia, we saw photos of flooding and trees down on the TV. Message when you can, and we'll talk once Veronica passes.

Good idea, love you. Big hugs to Elena and the twins xx

Misleading Dad feels wrong. Mia perches on the couch, wondering whether to call back. A branch flicks the window and she decides there's no point. He can't help and she doesn't want to worry him unnecessarily.

Karratha remains at Yellow Alert. Then at three p.m., a Red Alert is issued for the Hedland region, including Jude's property. The iron-ore port is closed, and large ships sent to sea to ride out the cyclone. The waves will be high out there, but at least the huge ships won't crash into anything.

With Port Hedland now officially in lockdown, Mia knows Mum can't come home, even if a chopper does become available. Winds of one hundred and sixty kilometres an hour are battering the coast and the latest reports show Veronica crossing south of Hedland, not far from Spinifex Downs. Mia bites her lip, trying to be brave.

Mum calls. 'Did you hear the news?'

'Yes, you're stuck there until the Red Alert is lifted!'

'Afraid so. Jude's neighbour sent a message via a SES worker. He'll chopper me home as soon as its safe.'

'Okay.' It's hard to hear Mum over the wind. 'We're still on Yellow Alert here, but I've checked the generator,' Mia shouts, 'and we have plenty of batteries for the radio.'

'Well done. If I can't call again, watch the sky after the alert lifts. Until then I'll be thinking of you.'

'Will do, love you!'

Mia texts Dad again to let him know she's safe, then hurries around the house, soothing the wallabies in the hallway, and trying to decide the safest room to huddle in when things become worse. She scans the yard. There's no sign of the horses. Sultan, Bandit and Freckles are still running free out there in the dangerous weather.

'Please be okay,' she whispers.

Rain belts down at bizarre angles as Mia plugs in her old headphones, singing along with her music as loud as she can to block the crashing cyclone sounds. She's exhausted her supply of sea-glass, so Mia puts away her wire and arranges the new earrings on the bench, ready to show Mum.

'I'll make a fortune at the next tourist market,' she tells Biff.

Late afternoon, Mia makes sure none of their windows or doorframes have rattled loose. Despite the slamming wind everything's still secure.

Her phone rings again.

'Hello.'

'Hi, it's Nick.'

'Hey, where are you – Karratha or Perth?'

'I'm back in Wickham.'

'What! I thought you'd be on a RFDS flight by now. Aren't they sending your dad to Perth?'

'Yep, he's on his way, but he needs me to stay here and look after the boats.' Nick pauses. 'And we were worried about you.'

'I'm okay.'

'I know you've got everything sorted.' Nick hesitates for a moment. 'But if you want company, I can come and help with the animals until Veronica passes.'

Mia looks through the bulging windows at the darkening sky.

'Is it still safe to drive?'

'Should be. We're not at Red Alert, but I reckon they might call it soon.'

'Thanks, Nick, that would be great. I'd love your help.'

'Okay, I'm on my way. See you in fifteen minutes.'

'The gate's open. I set the horses free after you left the other night. No need to close it.'

Mia clears up the kitchen while she waits. As car lights appear in the distance she breathes a sigh of relief. Nick toots as he reaches the yard and Biff runs to the door barking, then wagging his tail as he recognises the car. Nick rushes onto the veranda.

'Thanks for driving over.' She gives a shaky laugh. 'It's getting pretty scary.'

'No worries,' he yells, above the roaring wind. 'Wow, that branch made a mess of your stable. Lucky you set the horses free.'

'I know.'

As the storm slams the door shut behind Nick, Mia hears a high-pitched squeal.

'What was that?'

She presses her face against the windowpane, then grabs a torch. They ease open the door and peer into the driving rain.

'It looks like a horse.' Mia directs torchlight into darkness.

'Where? I can't see anything.'

'It's Bandit,' she cries, 'but where are the others?'

Bandit steps into the beam of light and Mia gasps. A twirl of barbed wire is tangled across his left shoulder.

'Oh, no, what's happened?'

The pony struggles towards them. Mia whistles and Bandit hobbles to the edge of the veranda. She takes his halter, steadying her breath so he won't take fright, and leads him over the sandbags and up the steps.

Bandit's eyes are wide with fear. Blood seeps from multiple wounds across his chest and one side. He needs urgent help, but Mia can't treat him on the veranda. She swallows. There's no choice.

Nick holds the door steady as she leads the pony inside the house.

Wind gusts send books and papers flying across the room. Biff runs towards them, barking.

'Get back,' Mia growls, and Biff jumps away, cowering in a corner. She rarely raises her voice to him, but right now, Bandit needs her full attention.

Each time the pony moves, sharp barbs twist and cut deeper. Bandit tosses his head, snorting in terror. Mia knows barbed wire can cause wounds so deep that horses die from blood loss.

'There now,' Mia soothes, 'there now.'

Nick grips the halter as she eases one hand along Bandit's flank, and Mia is grateful he spent so much time with their horses when his sister came to classes. As Mia's hand reaches the first barb, Bandit's nostrils flare. He shrieks and tries to rear.

'It's all right, fella, you know I just want to help.'

Mia moves her hand onto Bandit's neck, stroking and whispering until his breathing settles.

'Is it bad?' Nick asks.

Mia nods, wondering what Mum would do. She closes her eyes for a moment and the answer is clear. Mum would sedate Bandit, remove the barbed wire and then treat his wounds. But Mia has never sedated an animal, not by herself anyway. She's helped Mum plenty of times and knows what to do, but are kids even allowed to sedate animals?

Mia doesn't know, but someone has to do something and she's the only one who can. Contacting Mum is impossible. Jimmy might be able to help, he has experience healing horses – but if she calls Jimmy out in this weather, she could have two patients instead of one.

Mum usually treats horses on farms and stations; everything Bandit needs will be down in her surgery near the gate, where there's much more room to treat injured animals. The pony is losing blood. Mia has to make a quick decision. She can't take Bandit back into the cyclone. If he collapses halfway across the yard, they won't be able to move him and he'd die of exposure.

The pony shudders and his legs wobble. Mia decides to treat him in Mum's old surgery. It's not a large room, but it's safe.

'What can I do to help?' Nick asks as Mia drapes a light blanket across Bandit's chilled coat.

'Grab a sheet, towels and blankets from the linen cupboard,' she points across the room, 'and take them over to that room, the old surgery. You'll need to move the boxes off the floor. I'll need enough space in case Bandit lies down.'

'I remember your mum treating our old dog in here,' Nick says as he clears the boxes.

'Yep, before she built the new surgery by the gate.'

When Nick's finished, he takes the halter while Mia fills a bucket with water. Then she grabs hay from a bin on the back veranda. After so much time in a cyclone, Bandit needs food.

As Bandit begins eating, Mia says, 'I have to go out to Mum's new surgery.'

'What!'

'She keeps most of her equipment there now. I can't treat him without it.'

Mia makes a list of what she needs to bring back, remembering Mum's mantra: *Plan for any possibility. Having everything ready before a procedure is important.*

'If you keep Bandit steady and towel-dry the parts of him you can reach, that would be great.'

His warm brown eyes crinkle at the edges as she grabs a bag, turns on the torch and zips her coat.

'I'll be careful,' she tells Nick before he's able to say the words.

'You'd better be. I have no idea how to save him.'

The storm is strengthening. Flying debris slaps Mia as she slips and splashes across the yard. After treating Bandit, her legs will need antiseptic as well. She finds the equipment, then bolts back to the house.

'Thank goodness.' Nick closes the door behind her.

Bandit's eyes are wild. Mia lays everything where she can easily reach it. Then she takes the halter and explains what she needs to do. Nick follows her instructions. He's already spread a sheet across the floor. Mia gives him smaller sterile sheets to cover that. Then she opens one of Mum's equine treatment books.

Mia reads horse-weight-dosage charts, then checks the medicine she brought from Mum's vet fridge. The stronger drugs are kept in a locked box in the kitchen. Mum hides the key for safety but luckily Mia knows where it is. Her hands shake as she lifts the key, feeling like a criminal. Only trained vets are meant to dispense these drugs, but Bandit needs her. What else can she do?

Mia ignores the howling weather outside and forces herself to slow her breathing. If she gives the pony a wrong dose the outcome will be disastrous. As she disinfects Mum's strongest pliers and wire cutters, Bandit watches with terrified eyes. Mia prepares gloves, swabs, and an injection, lining them up in the order in which she'll use them, exactly as she's seen Mum do.

While Nick keeps the sterile sheet flat, Mia leads Bandit into position. He snorts at the strange smells and paws the floor, but she speaks softly. Human to animal, kind of like reverse equine therapy. At last Bandit stops shuddering and nuzzles her. His trust brings tears to Mia's eyes. She takes a deep breath, determined not to let him down.

After stroking Bandit's muzzle, Mia places a towel over the pony's eyes, so he won't see the syringe and panic. She checks the vascular chart to find the correct area, squashing her fear of missing a vein. Getting it right the first time is vital. She doesn't want to scare Bandit more.

Nick meets her gaze. 'You can do this,' he says.

She takes a deep breath, remembering how often she's watched Mum sedate animals, then she presses the stopper, injecting sedative into one of Bandit's largest veins. He tosses his head, struggling, but Nick holds the halter firmly. They watch Bandit's head lower as his respiration slows. Mia rests her forehead against Bandit's muzzle as his legs sway then spread wider.

Mia cradles his big head. The last thing she needs is for Bandit's weight to fall onto those vicious barbs! She monitors his breathing. The animal-size-to-medicine chart is only a guide; every horse is different. She needs him to be calm enough to treat, but not out for the count. It's a tricky balance. Mia watches carefully. She seems to have chosen the right dosage.

Mia strokes Bandit's neck as he settles, studying his terrible wounds and making a treatment plan. The first thing she'll have to do is cut away the wire and stop the bleeding. There are five deep gashes and dozens of smaller scratches. Each one will need to be cleaned. One barb is embedded so deeply, it might have cut close to the bone. She'll leave that one till last.

Bandit's steady breathing tells Mia it's time to begin. She pulls on operating glasses and thick protective gloves, then begins cutting the wire between each barb, making sure to protect herself and Nick each time it flicks away. Before removing any barbs, Mia carefully trims the wire around each wound, knowing that when she removes the barbs, blood could gush from the wounds. Bandit has already lost a lot of blood; now every drop is precious.

Mia changes the thick gloves for sterile medical gloves. She rinses Bandit's entire shoulder in antiseptic and turns to the least severe gash. Her hands tremble as she grips the pliers.

'Steady.' Nick's calm voice helps her focus. Mia closes her eyes for a moment, then begins.

Fifteen

||||||||||||||||||||||||||||||||||||||||||||||||||||||||||||||||||||||||||||||||

Blood spurts onto her face. Nick grabs a towel and wipes Mia's cheek as she puts the first barb into a bowl. She blinks, pressing gauze onto the cut, concentrating only on stopping the bleeding.

When the flow slows, Mia cleans the wound carefully, closes it with a butterfly clip, then smothers on antibiotic ointment. She covers the area with a dressing and wipes her face. So far, so good. She checks Bandit's heart and respiration rates, then repeats the process with the other three gashes, managing to stem the bleeding each time.

Mia knows the deepest cut will be the most challenging. As she pulls out that barb, they can see poor Bandit's bone.

'That must hurt,' Nick says, moving Bandit's mane out of the way.

She washes the deep wound, stems the bleeding, then peers at the gash again. Although the cut is deep, the muscles and tendons don't seem to be damaged.

Mia exhales and glances at the clock. There's not much time before the sedative wears off. Bandit will start to react soon. She doesn't want him to stumble and fall as he comes around.

'Why did I set you free?' She loops his mane around her finger. 'Would you have been safer in the stable?'

Nick shakes his head. 'Not after what happened to the roof . . .'

Mia remembers how Mum said freeing the horses would feel strange, but that they'd stick together and find somewhere safe. Bandit wasn't able to. Mia hopes Freckles and Sultan have.

'Imagining the worst won't help the horses,' Nick tells her, guessing where her thoughts have gone. 'Just focus on Bandit for now.'

She flexes her hands, knowing she'll need to conserve her strength. Bandit's recovery is going to be challenging, not only because of his size, but also because of his flight instinct. He won't like being inside.

Nick pours Mia a glass of juice. She takes a sip, then examines the last wound again. It's clean and no longer bleeding but it needs stitches, otherwise the gash will reopen as soon as Bandit moves. He can't afford to lose any more blood. Mia gathers her courage, preparing a needle and suture thread.

'You're doing a great job,' Nick tells her, but his face pales as she inserts the needle and it tugs Bandit's skin.

Horse hide is tougher than Mia imagined, way thicker than the skin of the wallaby that she and Mum stitched up last year. Mia has to push the needle harder than she expected. Nick looks away.

'I hope you're not going to faint,' Mia mutters.

He smiles sheepishly.

Mia focuses on cutting and tying each stitch. Sometimes Mum does continuous stitching, but that's way beyond Mia's skill level. She makes five stitches then, after she's finished sewing, stretches her aching hands and sits back to look at her work. She smiles. The wound is closed and her stitches are surprisingly straight.

Have I done everything the way Mum would have? She frowns. There's a niggling feeling that she's forgotten something.

Nick strokes Bandit while Mia makes sure he's completely dry, then they sit together waiting for the pony to come round. Mia chews her lip, worried about Sultan and Freckles.

'What if the other horses are lying in a paddock tangled in more wire?'

'They'll be right.' Nick squeezes her hand. 'What you did was totally brilliant.'

'Thank you.'

Mia wipes ochre-coloured mud from Bandit's legs, stroking another small scar on the cheeky pony's fetlock. Bandit tore the skin there a few months ago, jumping over a broken gate. It's healed well and he had a tetanus shot at the time. Thank goodness. Mum often tells her that rusty wire is a petri dish for germs. Mia's glad that tetanus is one thing she doesn't need to worry about.

Before Bandit comes out of sedation, they move as many things as they can. Mia doesn't want Mum coming home to a trashed room. It's past midnight and the pony will have to stay in the old surgery until first light, and maybe longer. They'll need to tether him, so while Nick rigs up a rope, Mia looks through the medicine chest, searching for natural ointments or a fast-working supplement to help keep Bandit relaxed. Something with valerian might help. She finds a herbal treatment Mum uses with anxious horses and reads the ingredients. It looks perfect.

Mia brings the medicine from the kitchen and notices Biff curled in the corner of the room, watching her with sulky eyes.

'Come on, you silly dog,' she calls, and Biff bounds across the room. 'I'm sorry for shouting. You know I love you!'

Biff wags his tail, then turns around and around in ecstatic circles.

Mia checks Bandit's breathing. It's deep and steady, a good sign. She strokes his head as the howling wind picks up another notch.

Suddenly there's an almighty bang. Mia turns to look out the window, then everything goes dark. Biff whines.

'It's okay,' she tells the kelpie, 'you know we're prepared for a blackout.'

Mia flicks on a torch, directing its beam to the emergency lanterns on the kitchen bench. Nick arranges them around the house. The soft light cheers her. It feels friendlier than electricity.

'Where's your generator?' he asks.

'There's a small shed off the back veranda, through

there. Here, take the torch, and good luck – the generator's a grumpy old beast.'

Nick steps around the hallway wallabies.

'You've got a full-on zoo in here.' He laughs.

'I know! Here.' She hands him a saucepan and spoon. 'Bang this as loud as you can when the generator's going and I'll flick the power changeover switch.'

'Okay.'

Mia feels for Bandit's pulse. The pony is still woozy. He should be more responsive by now. Did she give him too strong a dose? Mia shines torchlight onto the chart. The sedative amount was correct for his size.

'Come on, Bandit.' She takes his pulse again. 'You need to respond soon.'

Mia rests a hand on his neck, wondering what terrible things happened to him out there, and hoping the other horses are okay. She strokes his flank, trying to direct calm energy from her skin to his body. If humans can benefit from the sensitive, non-judgemental nature of horses, surely that also works the other way around.

Reverse equine therapy. Mia wonders if this is something other vets do. She'll have to ask Mum. In the meantime, Mia puts her arms around Bandit's warm, sweaty neck and breathes deeply. If someone made a perfume called Humid Horse, she would buy a dozen bottles.

While Bandit is calm, she checks the other animals by torchlight. The wallabies have livened up. They're bouncing off the walls again!

'You guys are ridiculous,' Mia tells the cheeky

teenagers. She's desperate to release them, but knows it's still too soon.

Mia hears the splutter and growl of the generator. She waits by the fuse box until she hears the saucepan clang.

'It's on,' Nick yells.

Mia turns the switch in the box from Mains to Generator. The lights flicker on and Nick darts back inside. He's soaked.

'I can give you a pair of Mum's baggy overalls and a T-shirt,' Mia offers.

Nick stifles a yawn as she goes to get them. He changes in the bathroom. The clothes fit pretty well.

'Cute possum in there.' Nick tries to smother another yawn as he walks back to Bandit.

'Why don't we take turns to nap?'

'I'm okay.'

Mia points to the couch. 'It's going to be a long night,' she says as she hands him a blanket, 'and who knows what will happen tomorrow.'

'Are you sure?'

Mia promises to call as soon as Bandit wakes up. She returns to Mum's old surgery and sits in a chair beside Bandit, stroking his neck. Before she knows it, Mia is also asleep.

Bandit shivers and she wakes, feeling like she's slept for ages. When Mia checks her watch she sees that it's been less than an hour. Bandit is staring at her, his eyes wide with surprise. Mia grins as he looks around. The pony has never been inside the house, what must he be thinking?

His legs twitch, and Bandit's eyes become suddenly panicked. His nostrils flare in terror.

'There now,' she says, over and over, until Bandit's eyelids droop and he dozes again. Mia wonders if that's normal.

She wriggles her cramped feet and checks the dosage chart again. Yep, the sedative was correct. Mia wonders what else she can do to revive him. Biff settles by Mia's side, keeping her company until Bandit begins moving again.

'Thank goodness,' Mia whispers.

Nick wakes and comes over as Mia rearranges the sheets and a bucket below Bandit, covering everything she can to minimise mess. She's barely finished when he pees. A lot!

He's missed the bucket, but Mia is relieved to see that Bandit's urine is clear. While Nick uses a rope to tether him to the wall rail, she mops the floor with an old towel. They pile hay in front of Bandit. He tosses his head then wobbles for a moment before seeming to accept that he can't turn to inspect his wounds, and that for now, he also can't go anywhere.

The roar of the cyclone is deafening. Mia stands at the surgery door, stroking Bandit to keep him calm.

'Well done,' Nick yells. 'I'm glad I didn't faint while you were stitching.'

'Thanks for all your help!'

Nick gives her a self-conscious smile. 'I don't suppose you have anything to eat? I'm starving.'

She pours cereal into two bowls. As they eat, Mia

watches Biff guarding the surgery door. There's a wary stand-off between dog and pony, each staring the other down.

'It's all right, Biff.' She goes over to pat him, then checks Bandit's pulse and temperature. He's doing okay.

They take turns monitoring Bandit and trying to doze. Neither of them gets much sleep with Veronica's fury bearing down on them. The bureau warns:

Cyclone Veronica is approaching the coast and displaying a very large eye. A prolonged impact is expected with extremely dangerous storm tides for parts of the Pilbara. Tides are already running high, and Veronica will force extra water onshore, resulting in significant coastal flooding. The biggest risk is at high tide; today at one p.m. and then again at one a.m. Rainfall in excess of 500 millimetres could cut roads and isolate communities, many of which have already lost power.

'This must be the slowest cyclone ever!' Mia groans. 'Hurry up and cross the coast, or turn and go back to sea for good.'

Branches slap angry replies across the roof.

At dawn Mia checks Bandit again. She strokes the whorl above her pony's eyes, then pulls back her hand. He's burning up. Mia grabs a thermometer and takes Bandit's temperature. The screen shows 39.2 degrees. She bites her lip, willing herself not to panic. Bandit nickers, then lies on the floor.

146

Screaming for Mum to help is useless, even though that's what Mia wants to do. Her mother is over a hundred kilometres away. Why did she let herself sleep when Bandit needed her?

She reaches for her phone to call Mum. It's flat. Mia forces her trembling hands to be still. She's the only one who can save Bandit; she has to stay calm.

'What would Mum do now?' Mia closes her eyes to concentrate.

Lower the patient's temperature, of course.

'How can I help?' Nick asks.

'Put this on charge,' she hands him her phone, 'then soak these towels in cold water.'

Mia lays wet fabric across Bandit's head and all along his side, ignoring his plaintive whinnying.

'Shhh, it's okay. This is for your own good,' she tells him.

Bandit looks exhausted and his rapid breathing shocks her. Mia thinks back to times she's helped at the surgery, remembering everything Mum does after operations. Mia can't think of anything she should have done differently.

Medical books are lined up on Mum's surgery shelves, but they're impossibly detailed. Mia's heart pounds as she flicks the pages back and forth, looking for a chapter about horse reactions to fever.

What have I forgotten? Then suddenly Mia realises. 'I didn't squirt antiseptic into the last wound before closing it, and I haven't given him antibiotics. No wonder Bandit's struggling!'

She jumps up and opens the fridge, grabbing the medicine she needs.

'Can you give it to him now?'

'Yes.' Mia reads the instructions carefully, then rips open the packaging. 'How stupid of me,' she mutters.

Nick grabs her trembling hands and holds them for a moment.

'You are doing a great job!' he reminds her.

Mia takes three deep breaths, then she splashes antiseptic across the deepest wound and injects the antibiotics. As Nick resoaks the towels, she wipes Bandit's muzzle.

'It's okay,' she tells the pony. 'You're going to be all right.'

Bandit's chin whiskers twitch. Mia loses all track of time as she strokes and sponges, too busy focusing on her patient to worry about Veronica's fury outside. Meanwhile Nick moves around the house, soothing the animals and checking each room. The wind is screaming like millions of frenzied cicadas, but the windows and doors are strong.

While Bandit battles his fever, Mia massages her aching muscles. For the first time, she understands the dangers for vets with strains and repetitive sprains. No wonder Mum tries to be so careful.

At last Bandit's fever drops and their hard work is rewarded with a soft whiffle. The pony gathers his strength and stands. He wobbles for a moment, then tosses his mane, nudging Mia gently.

'You're welcome,' she says, scratching his forehead.

Bandit's ears lean forward. He sniffs his hay, then begins nibbling with dogged determination. Mia laughs, knowing now that her beautiful pony is going to be okay.

Sixteen

||||||||||||||||||||||||||||||||||||||||||||||||||||||||||||||||||||||||||||||||

While Bandit eats, Mia checks each room. Their sturdy little house seems to have survived the peak of the cyclone.

Nick is desperate to get back to Point Samson to check their boats, but the Red Alert remains. He has to be patient. The bureau reports that Cyclone Veronica has stalled, circling about eighty kilometres off the Pilbara coast. The erratic cyclone is almost stationary while gradually, gradually weakening.

They peer into the yard. It's strewn with branches and all kinds of debris. Bandit is resting quietly, but the hallway wallabies are restless. Dodger boxes Mia playfully. Then he balances on his tail, showing off, until she scratches his chest.

'You are too cheeky!'

He bats his beautiful lashes and hops up and down the hallway. She cuts veggies for his gang and the wallabies crunch their carrots happily.

Mum calls and tells her the conditions are less severe now at Spinifex Downs.

'Hopefully they'll downgrade Veronica soon,' she shouts as the phone cuts in and out. 'Jude's neighbour is on standby, ready to bring me home . . .'

'I can't wait to see you, but don't worry. Nick came back to help me with the animals.'

'Thank goodness! Someone told Jude the old shade trees in Wickham have all come down. How are our trees?'

'Okay, I think.' There's no point telling Mum about the stable yet.

Mia looks across at Bandit. He's passing urine and pooping without any trouble. He seems to be out of danger and surely Mum will be home soon. She decides not to tell her about him either. She'd only worry.

By midafternoon, Mia is sure the cyclone intensity has shifted. She rests a hand on the windowpanes. They're not bulging as much as before. Nick turns on the radio. The cyclone warnings haven't changed but that's not surprising. With no weather stations on the peninsula, it's hard for the bureau to be exact. Conditions on one side can be totally different to the other. And forecasters always err on the side of caution. Mia crosses her fingers, daring to believe it might end soon.

Nick steps cautiously onto the veranda, then looks back at Dodger and his bouncy gang.

'Maybe it's safe enough to set the wallabies free.'

Mia peers out. The tortured trees seem less stooped, but the rain is just as intense. As Mia joins Nick, she's sure that she can sense a change. After days of build-up and coexisting with this yowling monster, it's as if part of Mia's own body is shifting. She can feel it in her skin. Maybe this is what Jimmy was talking about with insects and birds knowing.

The wallabies crowd around the screen door, gazing out.

Mia grins. 'You're right; let's free them. Dodger is driving me bonkers.'

She opens the back door and the wallabies hop into the rain without a backward glance.

'Yep, they were ready!'

The hours pass. As Veronica weakens Bandit continues to improve. It's frustrating to be stuck inside for so long. Mum calls again. The line is clear this time, so Mia tells her about Bandit.

'You've done an amazing job,' Mum says. 'Keep sending me updates.'

The wind lessens. They venture out onto the veranda and discover why the power went out. A massive tree has brought down their powerline. Live wire is flicking across the yard like a deadly snake.

'Lucky the tree fell after Bandit came home.' Nick runs a hand through his hair. 'If he'd stepped on those live wires, they could have electrocuted him.'

Mia stares at the coiled cables snaking around. The ground is soaked. She remembers the schools' annual flood warnings about electrocution risks. Puddles can conduct electricity, and half their yard is underwater. With two horses still to come home, she shudders at the thought of what might happen.

They need to alert the emergency services so they can deactivate the line. Mia calls the operator. He takes her details and logs the dangerous fault.

'Stay clear until we call back to confirm the powerline along your track has been isolated. Is the phone you're calling from the best way to contact you?'

'Yes.' Mia repeats her mobile number, then asks, 'If you isolate our line, will that affect our neighbour further down the track?'

'Probably.' The operator pauses. 'Emergency services will be in touch as soon as the line is deactivated.'

'Okay, thank you.'

Mia turns to Nick. 'I need to let Jimmy know via the UHF radio.'

Mia picks up the two-way receiver. Channels 5 and 35 are reserved for emergency messages. This *feels* like an emergency, but she decides to try a private line first. She selects their regular frequency. Mia listens to make sure no one else is using the channel, then pushes the microphone button.

'Hello, Jimmy, it's Mia. Can you hear me? Over.'

After a moment, Jimmy replies, 'Hearing you loud and clear, despite Veronica giving us what-for. Are you and Zara okay? Over.'

'Mum is still at Spinifex Downs . . .'

'Struth, are you all right, girly? Over.'

'I'm okay. Lorenzo's son, Nick, is here helping.

Lorenzo had an accident, but he's all right. That's not why I called, though. We have electrical wire down and two of the horses are free. I've called emergency services to isolate the line.'

'Good thinking, over.'

'But it means you won't have power . . .'

'No worries, I'll fire up the generator, over.'

'Thanks, Jimmy.'

'You said two horses, what about your third horse? Over.'

'Bandit is here. At the house. It's a long story, over.'

'Rightio, you sit tight and when the power goes out, I'll know the line is isolated and that you're safe.'

'Thanks, Jimmy.' Mia feels the tension ease from her shoulders.

'Anything else I can do?' Jimmy asks. 'Over.'

'Tell Veronica to hurry up and cross over or get back to sea!'

'Yep, she's the slowest darn cyclone I've ever known, but I reckon we're coming to the end of it, over.'

'The wind is still wild here – hopefully it'll start easing soon.'

'You stay strong, Mia, and say hello to Lorenzo's boy. I'm glad he's with you. Once it's safe, I'll get on over. Over.'

She thanks Jimmy again and lifts her chin. *Not much longer*, Mia thinks as she returns to Bandit. *We can get through this*.

An hour later her mobile lights up. It's the operator calling through with a message.

'All good,' he tells her. 'They've isolated your line.'

'Thank you.'

Mia and Nick talk about school, hatchlings and books. Like Mia, Nick's a reader. They like similar books. He asks her about the English speech and after lots of encouragement Mia agrees to read it.

'That's great,' he tells her as she finishes within the time limit. 'I love all the turtle references and the bit about the wildlife sightings map is important.' He shrugs. 'We all need to pitch in and fix up the mess our planet's in.'

The day drags on. They watch a movie, and as Veronica loses intensity, Nick paces the lounge room.

'I hope the boats haven't been damaged,' he tells her. 'I should have triple-checked the mooring lines before we left.'

By late afternoon the wind is even lighter, but reports from the bureau still don't reflect the change.

'It will be low tide soon,' Nick says. 'After that the floodwater will keep rising. What do you reckon, is it safe enough for me to drive as far as the bridge and see if it's passable?'

Mia looks at the sky. It's clearer, but she doesn't want to be the one to make that call. They listen to another weather report.

Hundreds of homes across the Pilbara are now without power. The slow-moving nature of Cyclone Veronica means there will be an ongoing impact, with SES workers unable to get out and help. Pilbara residents are advised to take care, stay inside and avoid creeks, rivers and coastal areas until they're sure that flooding is easing.

Nick decides to be cautious and wait till first light.

'Surely they'll have lifted the alert by then.' He stands on the veranda watching the clouds.

They feed the animals and settle down for the evening. Veronica's screaming voice has dropped to a low howl. The wind drops further during the night, but *still* there's no alert update.

At first light, Nick circles the veranda, scanning the sky.

'Almost low tide again,' he says as Mia brews a pot of tea, 'my best chance to get home. Are you okay here if I go?'

She nods. 'Bandit's on the mend and the power has been isolated. You started our grumpy generator for me and I still have plenty of food. I'm fine.'

'I'll drive to the bridge and make a decision there.'

'Don't cross if it isn't safe.'

His brown eyes smile. 'I won't.'

Mia cuts him a slab of cake and watches his car ease carefully down their driveway.

'Be safe,' she whispers.

Seventeen

||||||||||||||||||||||||||||||||||||||||||||||||||||||||||||||||||||||||||||

The strong tea gives Mia energy. Between sips she takes deep breaths, making a plan for the day ahead. By eight a.m. it's clear the cyclone has weakened, but Veronica is still hanging around just off the Pilbara coast.

'Just cross or go back to sea!' Mia shouts to the sky.

With the wallabies gone, her chores are easier, although caring for Bandit is still a challenge. She checks his wounds – they look clean. Bandit isn't well enough to go outside yet, but he does need some gentle exercise. Mia takes his halter and leads him around the house, doing laps of the lounge room.

Thankfully Bandit doesn't pee until he's safely back in Mum's surgery. She changes the sheets under the pony again, then checks that the wall tether is holding. It's fraying in a few places where Bandit has been chewing it, but for now, the tether is stronger than he is. She hopes that won't change.

Mia stretches, trying to decide what to do next.

Nick must be home by now. She hopes his boats have survived Veronica.

She fills her water bottle with drinking water from the bath. The level is lowering, but she's not sure how to hook the water pump to the generator. They'll need uncontaminated water until the electrical wire can be cleared and mains power returns.

Mia carries a large bucket into the yard to catch rainwater. She fills the possum's water sipper, then walks around the house, trying to get more than one bar of reception on her phone. She wonders what her friends are doing. Hopefully not texting with Erin. Mia tries to imagine how Erin and her family coped with their first big cyclone. If they had to drag debris from the yard, maybe those sparkly nails met their match . . .

After listening to music through her headphones, Mia switches on the radio in time to catch another weather update. There's still no news about Wickham or Point Samson, but with lines down and no weather bureau on the peninsula, that's not surprising.

Heavy flooding is reported between Jude's place and Roebourne, so the road north will be impassable for days, or maybe even weeks. Spinifex Downs was closer to the cyclone than their property. If the wind keeps dropping, Mum should be able to fly back soon. Mia crosses her fingers.

Being home alone is making her stir-crazy. She decides to tidy up and surprise Mum with a house that doesn't smell like a zoo. After wiping and cleaning for an hour, she takes a break to feed Roxy and the possum.

There are still a few blood splotches on the floor which Mia can't scrub off, so she covers the biggest stain with a rug from her bedroom, then sits on a chair beside Bandit, reading her book. Her pony looks fine, but still needs regular observations.

Her eyelids flicker, but she's determined not to fall asleep. She steps outside for fresh air and sees someone at the gate. It's Jimmy!

'Thank goodness,' Mia whispers, splashing across the yard. Jimmy's kelpie scampers over to greet them and Biff circles his friend. Their furry tails fan the humid air.

Jimmy holds up a bag of carrots and apples. 'I was worried you'd be running low on food for the animals,' he says. 'I came as soon as it felt safe.'

Tears fill Mia's eyes at his thoughtfulness. 'Thank you.'

Jimmy gives her a quick, awkward hug, then pats her shoulder.

'Where's Lorenzo's boy?'

'Nick went home early this morning. He was worried about their boats.'

Mia shows him the broken powerline, and they go inside. Jimmy puts the carrots and apples on the table. He looks around and sees Bandit's head peeping out from Mum's old surgery.

'Whoa, what's that cheeky horse doing inside?' Then he notices the bloodstained floor. 'Crikey, what's happened here?'

'Bandit ran into barbed wire, or maybe it blew onto him. He came home late Saturday evening with barbs caught across his neck and shoulder.'

'Poor fella.'

The old stockman goes to Bandit. He lays his hands near the pony's heart and closes his eyes. As Jimmy's hands move across Bandit's chest, Mia remembers his words about having a sixth sense, like the corellas and ants.

'You've done good work there, Mia. He's had a shock, but you've saved him. Your mum has taught you well.' He pats her shoulder. 'I reckon she'll be darn proud when she gets home.'

Mia can't help herself. His kind words make her burst into tears.

'There now, girly, there now,' Jimmy says, as she takes a few deep breaths, 'you've been so brave. We're over the worst of it now and that wind would scare the bejesus out of anyone, even those one-eyed Cyclops!'

Mia laughs, wiping her tears and realising that putting on a brave face is exhausting. What must Jimmy have gone through when he lost his beloved Elsie? Mia gives her neighbour a shaky smile, grateful in a weird way to have this new insight. It makes her feel stronger. And more determined to be kind to others.

'Thanks, Jimmy.' She suspects he's just as happy to see her after a couple of days alone. 'What about a cuppa?'

'Now, that's a beaut idea. Is your generator working?'

'Yep.'

Jimmy sips his tea and walks to the window. 'When did that branch come down on the stable?'

Mia shudders, remembering the crash. 'The other night, after Nick left,' she tells him. 'That feels like forever ago.'

'Lucky you set the horses free.'

'They galloped away as soon as I opened their gate, but now I'm worried they're out there tangled in barbed wire as well.'

'Worrying never does any good. If they're not home by midday tomorrow, I'll drive out bush and search.'

'I'll help . . .'

'No, the best place for you is here with the other animals. Bandit needs you more than they do, at least until your mum gets back.'

Mia walks across to give Bandit an apple. 'Mum's been offered a lift home by chopper as soon as it's safe.'

'Good.' Jimmy looks at the sky. 'Veronica's done. I don't know why they haven't lifted the alert, but once they do, your mum will be back. Maybe first thing tomorrow.'

He gazes out at the fading light. 'In the meantime, how about I make a start on chainsawing that branch? Then in the morning we can fix the stable roof, so the horses have somewhere cosy to canter home to.'

'Is it safe to chainsaw in the rain?'

'No problem for the chainsaw. I just need to be careful not to slip.' He points to his sturdy boots by the door. 'Don't worry, those old soldiers won't let me down.'

Mia watches Jimmy carve through the fallen branches with even, considered strokes and thinks, if he wasn't so kind, the old stockman could double for a stuntman in a horror movie. She sees how carefully he studies the wood before slicing, with his trusty boots grounding him safely in the mud. *Maybe Jimmy was a woodcutter when he was young,* Mia thinks, *before he became a stockman?* Then she realises that despite knowing Jimmy for years, she really doesn't know him at all. She'd like to change that.

Jimmy trims the wood into campfire-sized chunks, then stacks them into a pile. Mia watches him assess the damage to the roof before hobbling back to the veranda.

'Rightio, that's the first part done,' he says, drying himself with a towel.

'Thanks, Jimmy, that's amazing. I've still got some chicken curry in the fridge. How about sharing an early dinner?'

'That'd be bonzer. I'm sick to death of my own cooking!' Jimmy explains what else is needed to fix the stable. 'And the sooner it's done, the better,' he adds. 'You can't have that pony inside for much longer.'

Mia watches Bandit tossing his head. He's their most free-spirited horse and with his strength return-ing, it won't take him long to chew his way through the tether rope.

'My boots are old battlers as well,' she tells Jimmy, 'and I don't mind the rain. If you tell me what to do, I'm happy to get started. Maybe we can fix the roof before dark.'

'That's the spirit, girlie. Let's have a crack at it now, then enjoy your dinner afterwards.'

They drain their mugs of tea, gather the tools they'll need, and head outside. The dogs bound behind, splash-ing, and chasing each other through the mud.

'If we straighten this side beam,' Jimmy says, 'and repair what's left of the roof, the horses will have enough shelter to keep dry. Then when this wind eases, we can nail hessian over the gaps in the wall. After your mum's back, I'll come over and we can do a more permanent job.'

Mia steadies a ladder while Jimmy stabilises the roof and hammers down loose areas. As the dusky light fades into darkness, they head inside to wash up for dinner.

'I could eat a horse!' Jimmy jokes before looking across at Bandit and adding, 'Don't worry, not you, old fella.'

Mia piles a huge serve onto Jimmy's plate. There's a comfortable silence as they tuck into the curry. Jimmy eats everything on his plate, then sits back and pats his stomach.

'That's the best feed I've had in a long while.'

'You worked hard for it, and now the horses have shelter when they come home. *If* they come home . . .'

'Don't you fret. I reckon Sultan and Freckles will be galloping back very soon.' Jimmy calls his dog. 'Now, if you're okay here, we'd better skedaddle. Give me a hoy on the UHF if you need anything. If not, I'll drop by tomorrow morning to check that the stable roof is holding.'

'That would be great.'

Mia sleeps fitfully on the couch near Bandit. The night feels endless. She shivers when she hears the mournful cry of a curlew. The bird moans on and on, its voice like the cry of a terrified child. Some locals reckon that curlews foretell death. Mia moves closer to Bandit, listening for any changes in his breathing.

Normally Mia loves the isolation of their property, but right now she'd give anything to have someone here to talk to.

'I should have asked Mum to come home when she could still get through,' Mia mutters as she strokes Bandit.

She looks around the room, mind-listing five things she can 'see': Mum's riding boots by the door, a family photo on the bench, her jewellery making things, Biff's basket, lots of books. Now, what can she 'hear'; hmm, not the curlew! Mia moves onto three things she can 'touch'. Her favourite cushion, Bandit's mane, cool floorboards. By the time she gets to 'smell' her breathing is more relaxed.

As darkness drains into a stormy grey half-light, she boils water in a saucepan to make a cup of tea. Bandit is resting peacefully, so she carries it back to bed and stretches out more comfortably to wait for daybreak. Biff snuggles against Mia's toes, his tail giving an occasional lazy wag.

As dawn colours brush the grey clouds, Mia checks Bandit's temperature again. It's 38 degrees – normal.

'We did it.' She rests her head gently on his neck. Bandit turns his head and nuzzles her.

Although looking after him was terrifying, Mia's proud to have managed the challenge, with Nick's help.

Bandit and the other animals are safe. Well, most of them. Mia wishes she could have saved the old corella. And what about Freckles and Sultan? Have they made it through the cyclone?

Mia takes a bunch of grapes and sits on the veranda. The flooding has spread and there's no sign of the other horses. As she crunches fruit, Mia looks out at a lake where there used to be paddocks. The midges and mosquitoes will be terrible in the weeks ahead, but in five months' time, the August wildflowers are going to be incredible.

The storm clouds are still heavy and most of their yard is underwater, but the rainfall is definitely lighter. She splashes across to the stable to check the repairs. As Mia leans against the poles and taps the roof, water drips off the eaves into the channel she dug. Was that only last week? It feels like forever. The stable walls are sturdy and there's enough roof to protect Bandit, as well as his buddies, when they come home.

The wind has weakened, but before Bandit comes out the gaps in the wall need to have hessian nailed across them. Before she gets started, though, Mia needs a rest. She goes inside and washes Bandit's wounds with saline one more time. His wall tether is threadbare but still secure.

'Please stop chewing it!' she tells him.

He swishes his tail.

Mia checks Bandit's eyes and mouth. His gums are a healthy pink and his appetite has returned. The more hay Bandit eats the more cheeky and restless he becomes, but after what the pony has been through, eating as much as he can is important.

Mia piles up more feed, then collapses onto the couch. It's only midmorning but she's so tired. Her dream is peaceful. Wallabies and horses graze happily in paddocks of bright wildflowers. Corellas fly overhead in a brilliant blue sky. Mia sleeps deeply. Then a wet muzzle tickles her face.

Mia blinks and looks up. 'How come you're free?' she asks Bandit.

He whiffles in reply. Then Mia notices the smell. She wrinkles her nose and looks around. The tether is broken and a steaming pile of manure sits in the middle of the rug she brought out from her bedroom.

'Oh Bandit,' she sighs. 'You really need to be outside.'

Eighteen

Mia clips a lead rope onto Bandit's halter.

'Okay, buddy,' she says, 'it's time for you to go back to your stable.'

After smearing another dab of antiseptic cream over the line of stitches, Mia leads him onto the veranda. The pony lifts his head to smell the air. After a loud snort, he follows Mia across the yard, stepping warily through the hoof-deep water. Mia leads Bandit around the electrical wire. She knows it isn't live, but avoiding it altogether feels safest.

As they reach the stable, Bandit trots ahead of her. He peers around, steps up to his feed trough, then begins chomping hay.

'You're definitely on the mend,' Mia tells him as she checks the walls. 'And while you eat, I'm going to fix those gaps for you.'

Mia cuts hessian bags into small squares. Then she nails them across the holes in the walls. After making it snug, she steps back to assess her work. The patchwork looks strange, but it's blocking Veronica's final wind flurries.

Being outside feels great after being cooped up inside for so long. Mia gazes across the flooded paddocks. Their sandbagged house looks like a little island.

There's still no sign of Sultan and Freckles. She piles up more feed.

'Don't eat it all before the others come home,' she warns Bandit before going back to the house.

The manure smell in the lounge room is intense. Mia opens the western-facing windows, puts on gloves, then shovels Bandit's droppings into a bucket. She carries the dung to the compost pile, then goes back to collect the stinky rug. She hangs that over the nearest fence. The patchy rain isn't heavy enough to wash it, so Mia hoses away the muck. She doubts the rug is salvageable, but it's her favourite – worth a try.

Her next job is checking the helipad. The platform is well above the flooded part of the yard and the landing circle is mostly clear of debris. Now that the wind is so light, Mum and the pilot can easily land safely. As long as they're able to take off from Spinifex Downs.

Mia scans the sky. There are no helicopter specks on the horizon. As she walks back to the house, Mia hears crackling. It's the UHF transmitter.

'Are you there, Mia? Come in, Mia. It's Jimmy, over.'

She hurries in and lifts the receiver.

'Hello, Jimmy, it's Mia, over.'

'Thank goodness, girlie, you had me worried when there was no answer! Over.'

'Sorry, I was patching the stable walls and checking the helipad.' Mia decides Jimmy doesn't need to know about Bandit's manure mishap.

'Good for you. Everything okay? Over.'

'Yes, over.'

'Any sign of your mum?'

'Not yet.'

'The horses? Over.'

'Also not yet.'

'They won't be too long now. How's the stable? Over.'

'Your repairs are holding. I had a go at nailing hessian patches over the walls. They look a bit weird, but they're blocking the wind. Bandit's out there now, hoovering up hay.'

'Crikey, you're a little legend. Well done! Over.'

Mia grins. 'I'm not sure how long my repairs will last. Over.'

'If they hold until tomorrow, that'd be beaut. I'll be there late morning to do more repairs. Over.'

'Thanks, Jimmy. Do you have enough food until then?'

'Plenty, but nothing as good as that chicken curry! Over.'

'When Mum's home, let's share dinner again. She makes the best fish curry.'

'You're on. Stay safe in the meantime. Don't take any risks. Over.'

'Okay.'

Her stomach grumbles as she hangs up. Breakfast feels like a long time ago. She gives Biff a doggy treat, then checks out the remaining food. There's still an avocado. She could add that to corn chips and canned beans to make nachos.

Mia arranges the food into layers then smothers it all in sour cream, grateful that the backup generator is still keeping the fridge going.

While she crunches her meal Mia listens to the midday weather report.

Cyclone Veronica has now weakened to a Category One system after pummelling the Pilbara coast for twenty-four hours. Destructive winds have damaged buildings and brought down powerlines. Wind speeds of 155 kilometres were recorded east of Roebourne, with wind gusts up to 220 kilometres. The cyclone did not make landfall, but has dumped hundreds of millimetres of rain across the region.

'Sounds like Mum and Jude copped the worst of it,' Mia tells Biff. 'I hope they won't get flooded in.'

Conditions in Port Hedland have eased, but warnings remain for areas west of Port Hedland to Mardie. Veronica is now tracking westwards parallel to the coast. It is expected that the system will continue to weaken further this afternoon. Schools remain closed.

That's one bonus, Mia thinks.

She takes her plate to the sink and looks out the window, glad their home is on high ground. The rain is patchy and the floodwater around their building has steadied. It might even be receding. Spinifex Downs is near Port Hedland, so if people there are allowed to leave their houses, surely Mum should soon be able to leave the cattle station.

She sprawls on a chair on the veranda, swinging her legs and watching clouds skid across the sky. In the distance, Dodger and his wallaby mates bound across the drenched paddocks. They look like they're having fun. Mia wonders whether the old bungarra is okay. Probably – that goanna must have lived through plenty of cyclones. It would have a safe hiding place somewhere.

After so much drama, doing nothing but cloud-watching is peaceful. She watches faces form then dissolve into new shapes.

Mia rests her arm on the railing and notices that the ants are on the move again. Squadrons of them are marching purposefully along the veranda with tiny white pupas in their jaws. Even if Veronica has not been officially downgraded, the wild creatures are telling her that now she's safe.

'I did it,' Mia whispers to the ants. 'I got through a cyclone without Mum.'

As the insects march on, Mia wonders what her friends are doing and whether they're safe. She checks her phone; there are two bars at last! She tries to call Kirra but it goes to voicemail.

The clouds shift into faster-moving shapes. Then Mia sees a strange white cloud. It's dipping back and forth below the heavier rainclouds. As she watches it race towards her, Mia realises that it's not a cloud, but a gigantic flock of birds. She jumps up. The corellas are returning!

Excited squawking fills the air as hundreds of birds fly overhead. Mia laughs when the flock splits and their own resident birds leave the larger group, swooping down to circle their home property. They settle in their roosting tree and Biff races towards them. His tail doesn't stop wagging as he splashes around and around the tree. The little white birds ignore his barking, too busy hopping up and down the branches, arguing over the best places to perch.

There's still no sign of the horses, but a colourful haze follows the corellas. This time, it's a huge flock of green and yellow budgerigars whirling through the sky. Mia tries to guess how many birds there are; maybe a thousand or more? She closes her eyes to listen as high-pitched chirping fills the air.

Their calls remind her that there's still one more job that needs to be done. Mia's been putting it off until the rain eased.

'C'mon, Biff.'

She grabs the shovel and they squelch back the short distance to a little hill behind the house. Mia climbs up to a garden of rocks with painted names; Bill the Budgie, Bob the Blue-tongue, and many others. Mia chooses an area between the graves of two beloved rescue dogs and digs a hole. Then she goes back to collect the corella from the freezer.

'Sleep well, old corella.' She bows her head and

sprinkles a handful of seed over the bird. Then she fills the grave with muddy red dirt.

'Let's go, Biff.'

The kelpie trots obediently behind her as they head back to the house. Biff knows better than to dig here.

Bandit is resting comfortably, so Mia spends the rest of the afternoon checking her phone for reception and waiting for Veronica to be downgraded so that Mum can come home. Listening to weather reports helps pass the time.

Pilbara residents have now begun mopping up. After the Town of Port Hedland received the all-clear, crews have been able to assess damage to electrical infrastructure and begin restoring power. In some affected areas, including South Hedland, Wickham and much of Point Samson, power has been restored. Other homes in Karratha, Point Samson and Roebourne remain without power.

Mia knows their home line has been isolated, but she checks their power, just in case. It's still off. The yard is safe.

Veronica is set to weaken further today and will likely be downgraded to a low this evening. While the wind conditions are easing, with continuing rainfall in many areas, the Bureau of Meteorology reports that flooding is now the main concern for authorities.

The Red Alert is still in place. Mia knows Mum probably can't leave Spinifex Downs until it's lifted. The thought of another night alone makes her feel weepy, then angry.

'Why aren't they downgrading it?' Mia shouts at the radio as the afternoon shadows lengthen and the Red Alert remains. 'The wind has stopped!'

At dusk Mia stops watching the sky, knowing Mum won't get home today.

Biff and Mia eat a simple meal on the veranda and then curl up together on her bed.

'Not long now,' she tells the kelpie. 'One more night, then we'll all be together again.'

Nineteen

The corellas begin screeching at first light, and they keep on squabbling.

'It's too early to be so loud,' Mia mutters, hiding her head under the sheet, but a part of her is happy the birds are back. Hearing them squawk in the roosting tree makes things feel normal.

Biff jumps up.

'It's also too early to chase birds,' Mia tells him, but when she peers out from under the sheet, she sees Biff sitting still, ears raised, listening.

Mia sits up too.

Then she hears a steady *thwump, thwump, thwump*. It isn't the generator. Mia throws on shorts and a T-shirt, and runs onto the veranda. A shiny speck appears in the distant sky. She holds her breath and crosses her fingers.

'Please be Mum.'

The speck grows bigger. It's a chopper, and it's heading her way.

Mia steps into her boots and runs to the helipad.

Besides a few branches, the landing circle is still clear. She brushes them away and steps back.

Jude's neighbour swoops the property, then, seeing Mia by the helipad, dips and twirls around. Mia's hair flicks across her face as she looks up, shielding her eyes against the morning glare. Mum is sitting in the passenger seat, waving both hands and grinning.

The chopper lands. Mum grabs her medical bag, then ducks below the rotor blades and runs across the helipad into Mia's arms.

'I missed you so much!' Mia says, not even trying to stop her tears.

'Me too. We left Spinifex Downs as soon as we could.' Mum holds Mia close. 'Thank goodness you're all right.'

They wave as the pilot takes off again. Then, arm in arm, they wade to the house. Mia gives Mum a quick update about what's happened, and they go to the stable to check Bandit.

'Oh, my stars.' Mum examines his wounds. 'You poor fellow. What happened out there?'

'Barbed wire,' Mia mutters, before listing every step of his treatment. 'Bandit's fever was really high. He seems okay now, but I hope there's no infection.'

Mum finds a thermometer in her medical bag and takes the pony's temperature. Then she checks his eyes, heart, mouth, and smiles at Mia. 'You've done so well, darling. Bandit is out of danger and doing fine.'

Mia lets out a deep breath and points to the wound. 'My first stitches!'

'They're beautiful.' Mum hugs Mia for the longest

time. 'Chip off the old block! I'm so sorry you had to go through that alone. I should have come home earlier. Jude and Arrow needed me, but so did you.'

'It's all right. If you'd come home earlier, Jude's horses would have died.' Mia pauses. 'But I have thought of a plan for any more wet season emergencies.'

'What's that?'

'Next cyclone season we could ask Jimmy to stay in the house with our animals and you can take me along as your assistant.'

Mia watches Mum, hoping that she'll take the idea seriously.

'That's not a bad idea.' Mum ruffles Mia's hair. Then she asks, 'Were you very frightened?'

'Terrified,' Mia admits, 'but I had plenty of jobs to keep me busy. Biff was with me and I was relieved when Nick arrived.'

'You saved Bandit because you didn't panic. That's such an important thing for a vet.' Mum smiles. 'And you were brave!'

'I wasn't brave when Dad called . . .'

Mum looks stern as Mia explains about misleading him.

'I was going to call Dad back,' Mia says, 'and tell him you weren't here, but then there was no reception and now there's probably no point. He'd only worry if he knew.'

'Maybe . . .' Mum replies.

Mia sighs. She knows that Mum's 'maybe' means she thinks Mia should have been honest with Dad from the start.

'Once we have better reception I'll call him,' Mia promises.

'How's the possum?' Mum asks as they wade back to the house.

'It's been sleeping most of the time. The injuries look like they're healing.'

Mum examines the possum. 'You're a lucky little fellow.' She smears antiseptic over its deepest scratches. 'Once a cat gets one of you guys, not many live to tell the tale.'

Mum washes her hands and offers Mia a freshly baked scone from her daypack. 'That's from Jude. Sorry it's a bit squashed. Now, is there any food left for brunch? I'm starving.'

'It's a bit random.' Mia puts tomatoes, crackers, tinned fruit and muesli onto the bench. 'That yummy casserole is long gone, but there's still half a quiche. Jimmy and I ate all your chicken curry. He loved it. I said we could have him around for fish curry one evening.'

'Good idea.'

As they eat, Mia asks, 'Do you think Sultan and Freckles will be okay?'

'They've been through plenty of cyclones before.'

'Did any go on for this long?'

'Probably not,' Mum squeezes her hand, 'but they're smart horses.'

Mia is writing *I'm so grateful the helicopter pilot got Mum home* in her journal when they hear steps on the veranda.

'Cooee,' Jimmy calls. 'I saw the chopper.'

'Come in.'

'Stay,' Jimmy tells Dog, before taking off his muddy boots and joining them at the table.

'You made it,' Mia says, smiling.

'Slow and steady.' Jimmy hangs his hat by the door.

'Wading up that track won't be good for your hips,' Mum tells him.

'I'm fine. The doc said exercise is good for me.'

'In moderation!' Mum freshens the teapot and gets another cup. 'How are things at your place?'

'Not too bad. Branches and shrubs everywhere, but Elsie's frangipani tree survived, so that's the main thing.' He scratches his head. 'I don't remember any other cyclone going on for that long. Veronica didn't cross the coast, but she got a bit hairy there for a while.'

'She sure did. Thanks for helping Mia while I was gone. I'm so glad you were nearby.'

'*I* was glad *Mia* was nearby! She's darn level-headed in a crisis.'

'She is.' Mum offers him some tomato and crackers. 'Help yourself, Jimmy. I wish we had something better to offer, but our supplies are dwindling.'

'No worries, a cuppa will do just fine. I'm down to an orange, tuna and crackers at my place, but now that Veronica's passed, we'll be able to get into town soon.'

'And I hear you're coming over for a fish curry.'

Jimmy rubs his belly. 'My word, that other curry was good.'

Mum smiles.

'Are your horses back?' Jimmy asks.

Mia shakes her head.

'Once this floodwater drops, I'll go out in the ute and look for them.'

'Thanks,' Mum replies. 'I don't want to leave Mia and Bandit again.'

Jimmy nods. 'How about I keep working on that shed of yours in the meantime?' he suggests. 'Then it'll be snug when the horses do return.'

Mum pulls on her boots. 'How about we get stuck into fixing it together?'

'Rightio.'

As they head for the door, Mia's phone rings.

'It's Kirra,' she shouts.

Mum smiles at Mia. 'Why don't you stay here and chat with her while Jimmy and I work on the shed?'

Mia hugs Mum, then settles on the couch with her feet up on a cushion.

'You answered,' Kirra cries, 'at last!'

'Reception has been dodgy.'

'That's what we thought. Are you okay?'

'I am now that Mum's home.'

'When did she get back?'

'About an hour ago.'

'What! Have you been alone all this time?'

'Mum had to stay at Spinifex Downs. There was a problem with the foal. But then Nick came after his dad was airlifted to Perth.'

'What!'

Mia starts at the beginning.

'Weren't you scared?'

'Yes.'

'Me too, and I had my family!' Mia laughs as her friend continues. 'I can't talk for long, my battery is almost flat, but I want to hear all the details later. Jess and I have been trying to call you all day . . .'

Mia feels suddenly warm inside. They talk for a few more minutes before Kirra says, 'My phone is on red. I'll message again when it's charged.'

'Sure.'

A few minutes after Kirra hangs up, Jess sends a text.

Glad u r ok!

Same.

Were u really alone all that time?

Yes ☺

OMG I can't wait to hear about that. It's crazy in town. Big trees down everywhere.

Did anyone go to school 2day?

Don't think so.

U going tmrw?

Prob. Have 2 go now. Mum's making me mop!

Let's chat 2night.

☺ ☺

Being back in touch with her friends is the best.

Mia puts down her phone and races out to the stable.

After a couple of hours the repairs are finished and the stable is cosy again. Now all they need are the horses.

'I'll be off,' Jimmy says, 'and start searching for them on that back trail. It's above the flood level, so they might be sheltering there.'

'Don't get bogged.'

'I won't.'

Now that things have settled, Mia knows it's time to call Dad. He answers immediately.

'Mia, thank goodness. Are you okay? We've been so worried. How are you doing?'

'I'm good, Dad. The wind has dropped and besides a flooded yard, everything is fine.'

'Thanks for your texts Saturday night. When we didn't hear from you again we guessed there were problems with reception. We've been watching cyclone images on TV. The reporters said it's really unusual that Veronica stalled off the coast for that long. It must have been frightening.'

'Mmhmm, it was, and Dad, there's something I probably should have told you earlier . . .'

After Mia owns up to being alone during the first part of the cyclone, it takes Dad a while to settle down long enough to hear the details. Mia can hear Elena in the background telling him to stop talking and listen.

Meanwhile, Mum taps a text message into her phone and holds it out to show Mia.

Hi, it was my fault entirely. Our daughter was brilliant. We're busy with the animals and mopping up at the moment. Can I call later and explain?

'How about I send this to Dad?' Mum whispers.

Mia smiles and nods. After a quick ping, Mia hears Dad take a deep breath.

'Okay, cara mia, you're safe and that's what matters.'

'Thanks, Dad. I'm really sorry, I should have told you earlier.'

'Yes, your mum and I can talk about that later, but now, tell me what you did that was so brilliant . . .'

'Mum's exaggerating.'

'I doubt that.'

Mia laughs as Mum raises her eyebrows. Then she tells Dad about stitching Bandit's wounds.

'Brava! You are amazing.'

'I don't think you'll need to talk to Dad,' Mia tells Mum as she hangs up. 'He seems okay with everything now.'

'That's a relief,' Mum says, 'but I'll still call him later.'

As they clear fallen branches from the yard, Mia notices Mum scanning the paddocks, searching for some sign of their horses.

'I might go and have a rest.' Mum rubs her eyes. 'I didn't get much sleep at Spinifex Downs.'

'Okay.'

Mia sits in the stable with Bandit. She's combing his mane when his ears suddenly prick up. Bandit whinnies, then runs outside. He circles the yard, snorting in excitement.

Mia gazes across the floodwater. Two horses are cantering towards her. A small one and a tall one.

She runs to the house. 'Mum, I can see Freckles and Sultan. They're coming home!'

Mia remembers Mum's words and doesn't need to be told what to do. *When they return, they'll be chilled and hungry.* She checks their food, then grabs a towel ready to start drying them.

Freckles trots straight to her feed bin and begins

eating like there's no tomorrow. Sultan rubs noses with Bandit, then does the same.

'Thank goodness you're safe.' Mia's voice falters as she dries Freckles.

Mum tops up the feed troughs with oats and throws blankets over the shivering horses. She begins a careful examination, starting with their hooves and legs.

Sultan seems okay, but Freckles's leg muscles are twitching. While Mum takes the pony's temperature, Mia remembers how she calmed Bandit. She rubs the pony's chest with a towel, all the while whispering softly. At last Freckles stops shivering. The pony nuzzles Mia, then refocuses on eating hay as quickly as she can. Mia clips a coat over Freckles's little back, then adds another blanket over that. She turns to watch Mum examining Sultan.

'What can I do to help?'

'Check he's dry, then rub his chest the way you did with Freckles.'

Mia smiles. Reverse equine therapy isn't something she's imagined – she *can* calm horses. Like they calm humans.

She stands on a chair to make sure every part of Sultan is dry, clips on his warmest coat, then rubs the big horse's chest. He gobbles hay as she calms him, turning every now and then to nudge her.

'They're both fine,' Mum says, stepping back at last. 'Once that food warms them they'll probably just want to rest.'

Mia calls Jimmy on the UHF line to let him know the horses are safe, then returns to the stable to sit with them.

Nick sends a text. His dad has had surgery and hopes to return next weekend. Lorenzo won't be able to work on the boat for at least six weeks.

'I'm stepping in for him in the meantime,' Nick says.

'Great! How are the boats?'

'Besides a few scrapes, they weathered the cyclone really well. There's barely any damage.'

They chat for a while, then Mia leaves the horses to rest. She spends the evening watching a movie and texting her friends.

R u guys going to school?

No!

Me neither. Parents worried about floodwater ☺ ☺ ☺

'Mum,' Mia calls. 'No one's going to school tomorrow. Can I stay home?'

'What do you mean, no one? The alerts are lifted.'

'Jess and Kirra aren't going, and they don't know anyone else who is. I reckon most people will be busy cleaning up.'

'Do you have any tests or assignments due?'

Mia shakes her head. 'Only my English talk, and we won't do those until everyone is back.'

'Okay, darling. I reckon you've earned a day off.'

Twenty

|||||||||||||||||||||||||||||||||||||||||||||||||||||||||||||||||||||||||||||||||||||||||

Mia wakes to the sound of Biff's doggy door swinging as he runs out to chase corellas. She sits up and looks at the X taped onto her window. That can come off now.

After checking her phone for messages, Mia reaches for her gratitude journal and writes *I'm grateful our horses are home safely.*

'I've made pancakes with lots of maple syrup,' Mum calls from the kitchen.

'Yum.'

They listen to the news as they eat.

… while some inland properties, like Warrawagine, were grateful to get their first rain for the year from Cyclone Veronica, other coastal properties were inundated. Some cattle stations received well over 400 millimetres of rainfall, and pastoralists are carrying out aerial surveys, looking for cattle bogged in mud.

'Poor animals,' Mia says.

'I might be called out to help,' Mum warns her, 'or to euthanise the cattle that can't be saved.'

'That would be horrible.'

'It would,' Mum agrees, 'but it's better than leaving them to suffer.' She hands Mia bottled peaches to spoon over her pancakes. 'Whatever happens, I promise there won't be any more overnight call-outs this wet season!'

'Good!'

'And if rescuing bogged cattle wasn't such a horrible task, we could put your plan into action.'

'What plan?'

'The one about you assisting me while Jimmy minds the menagerie.'

Mia grins, excited that Mum has taken her offer seriously. 'I've saved enough patients for one week,' she says. 'I'm happy to leave bogged cattle to you.'

'No worries.'

Mum glances at the clock. 'The Wickham emergency workers sent a message earlier. They're coming to fix the powerline and should be here any minute.'

The breeze is still flicking the wire about the yard, so Mia's relieved to see a truck pull up near the fallen line.

'Thanks for coming so early,' Mum says, pouring them a cuppa.

'No worries. We've restored power to the rest of Wickham. Good that your daughter alerted us. That wire could have been deadly.'

'She's a smart girl.'

Mia blushes as the SES crew gulp hot tea, then get to work.

It doesn't take long. After the repair crew leaves, Mia shows Mum her latest sea-glass creations.

'You've been busy.'

'But now I've run out of glass. Seeing as the road to Point Samson is open, and I'm not going to school, maybe we could go and collect some? After that massive tidal surge there'll be heaps of good pieces on the high-tide line.'

'That's a lovely idea and I can make banana bread to drop off for Nick and his family. Unless there's still a loaf in the freezer?'

'No,' Mia replies. 'Biff and I ate it.'

'Of course you did.' Mum laughs and begins mashing thawed bananas.

Although the flooding has eased, Mum drives carefully, not taking any chances on the soft, muddy edges of the road.

'I hope Nick is home,' Mia says as they turn into his street. 'He might already be at the harbour.' Then she sees Lorenzo's new car parked in the driveway. As Mum pulls in behind it, Nick waves from the window.

'Nice wheels,' Mum says when Nick opens the door.

'Dad's business is going well,' Nick grins.

'How's his arm and foot?'

'Much better, thanks. He's flying home with Mum and Lexi on Saturday.'

'Here's a welcome-home snack for them.' Mum hands Nick the banana bread. 'And please tell Lexi we'd love to see her at equine sessions.'

'Thanks.' Nick holds the loaf to his nose. 'This smells amazing. I'll try not to eat it before they arrive!'

Mum laughs. 'I can always make more.'

'We've come to look for sea-glass,' Mia tells him. 'There's heaps along the high-tide line.'

'Well, you're probably busy,' Mum says. 'We won't stay.'

'That's okay. I don't need to be at the harbour for another hour. Come in, I'm making coffee. It's ready to pour.'

Mum sighs as she smells the roasted beans. She can't say no to the best espresso on the peninsula. Lorenzo has taught his son the old ways, and a pot is brewing on the stove. Nick pours coffee into a mug and shows Zara a photo of Lorenzo's arm and foot.

'Dad sent this. He said he's healing really well, thanks to Mia.'

Mum beams with pride while Mia turns a bright shade of beetroot.

'It's good that you came out this morning,' Nick continues. 'Something horrible has happened.'

Nick's a practical guy and Mia's only seen him this rattled when she stitched Bandit's deepest wound.

'What's wrong?' Mum asks.

'Cattle have washed up on the beach. Have you got time for me to show you?'

'Of course. Are they all right?'

Nick shakes his head. 'Here, take this,' he hands Mum the mug, 'I've made it strong. You might need it.'

They cross the road and hurry down to the beach.

'Oh, my stars,' Mum gasps.

Dead cattle are strewn across the sand, head to tail to leg to rump. Their big red bodies are twisted into strange angles, like distorted jigsaw pieces. Mia closes her eyes. She focuses her thoughts and manages her breathing. To her surprise she suddenly feels lighter. Mia opens her eyes and looks around. Nick takes her arm while Mum checks each bloated animal. There's nothing she can do for them now.

'Station owners said their cattle were swept out to sea,' Mum says as she looks around the beach, 'but we didn't expect them to end up here. Poor things.' She checks the beasts for branding or an ear tag. 'There's nothing to say which station they're from. I'd better call the shire ranger.'

'He's on his way,' Nick tells her.

Mia gazes at the nearest cow. Her eyes are open, and she looks strangely peaceful.

'Dozens of fish washed up as well,' Nick says. 'And there's a stingray over there.'

'Dead?' says Mia.

Nick nods.

'I hope our turtle hatchlings were far enough away to survive.'

'They'd have been long gone,' Nick reassures her.

Mia smiles at him, and this time it's Nick's turn to blush.

While Mum goes to the carpark to wait for the ranger, Nick helps Mia collect sea-glass. There are dozens of pieces in all shapes, sizes and colours, even blue.

'How are things going with the boat?'

'Great. This morning I'm taking a group of insurance guys to assess damage. Then tomorrow some scientists are coming down from Hedland to study the effects of "cyclonic coastal inundation". We'll go into some of the smaller estuaries to do that.'

'Watch out the scientists don't get taken by crocs.'

'Yep, the salties will be on the move after that huge tide.'

Mia scuffs the sand. There are so many great pieces of glass.

'Then I need to get ready for Dad's regulars,' Nick continues as they fill a bag, 'the oyster farmers and that mob who are monitoring coral trout numbers. There's plenty to do. It's full-on but I'm loving it.'

'What about school?'

'The teachers are going to send me assignments to do from home. They're being really supportive.'

Mia picks up a beautiful chunk of blue glass.

'That's a good one. What will you make it into?'

'I don't know. It's too big for an earring.'

'Maybe a necklace.'

'Hmm, good idea.' Mia holds it below her collarbones. 'I haven't tried that before.'

A pair of white-breasted sea-eagles circle the beach as Mum leads the ranger onto the sand. He takes photos of each cow, then Mum helps him chain the cattle to his car and drag them off the beach.

'Need help?' Nick calls.

'Nah, we're right.'

Nick picks up another chunk of glass and asks, 'When's your flight to Perth?'

'The day after school breaks up. Mum's driving me to the airport once we finish Saturday sessions.'

Nick checks his watch. 'I'd better head over to the harbour and get the boat ready for those insurance guys.'

'Hope it goes well.'

Mum and the ranger are busy with the cattle, so Mia texts Jess and Kirra while she waits.

I'm at Pt Samson with Mum.

How come?

Sea-glass collecting.

Fun!

Mia and her friends message back and forth. She tells them about the cattle then fills another bag with sea-glass. When Mum finishes, Mia shows her the beautiful chunk of sea-glass.

'Wow, what are you going to do with that?'

'I'm not sure, maybe make it into a necklace.'

'I have an old chain I never wear. You could use that.'

'Thanks.'

They drive home and find the horses waiting to meet them at the gate. Mia hugs them, so grateful they all survived the cyclone.

After lunch she spreads sea-glass across the kitchen table and drills a hole through the top of the big piece of blue glass. Mia adds a necklace mount, then threads it onto Mum's chain. She puts it around her neck, looks in the mirror and smiles. Who needs a French braid and acrylic nails when she has this?

Biff barks and runs to the door. Mia follows him outside.

'Hi, Jimmy.'

'G'day. Bonzer news about your horses. Are they all okay?'

'Yes, come and see. They're probably still eating!'

'Where were you cheeky fellas hiding for so long?' Jimmy mutters as he strokes the horses with his calloused hands.

'You were right about animals knowing things we don't,' Mia tells him. 'Once the ants and birds returned I knew I was safe.'

'You can't go too far wrong if you watch the wild creatures.'

After Jimmy heads home, Mia practises her persuasive speech one more time. She reads aloud, timing herself with a stopwatch.

'We were told to choose one issue and I decided on climate change . . .'

She takes another deep breath, telling herself not to gabble before beginning her explanation about sand temperature determining whether turtle hatchlings are male or female. She hopes everyone will be as surprised as she was to hear about turtle feminisation.

Mia continues reading, ending with, 'If we each choose a problem and take steps to improve things, we can all make a difference.'

She checks the time: four minutes, forty-one seconds. Perfect! It's a good argument and she knows she can deliver it within the time limit. That'll help settle her nerves when she stands in front of the class.

'Great speech,' Mum says. 'I reckon you'll do really well tomorrow.'

'Hope so.'

Twenty-one

Mia jumps out of bed. This morning she'll see her friends in person after only texting for so many days. She hopes it won't be weird. Mia still wonders what happened while she was out of range. Were they phone-chatting with Erin? And if they were, what was Erin saying about her?

Mia squashes the negative thoughts. She's tired of second-guessing everything. Kirra and Jess are her besties; they'll work it out.

And today is the persuasive speech. Soon that'll be over and done with. Her phone pings.

Good luck with your speech.

She sends a reply message to Dad with love hearts and horse faces. Then he sends a starry-eyed face in return. Mia laughs and puts away her phone.

'I'll pick you up after school if you like,' Mum offers. 'I'm going to the rescue centre in the afternoon. There might be animals that need help.'

'That'd be great.'

She finishes breakfast, pulls her hair into a ponytail and grabs her speech notes.

'Ready?' Mum asks.

Mia nods. She's practised so many times. Now all she needs to do is say the words on her palm cards and appear confident.

'When you're doing your speech,' Mum stands taller, 'channel your inner cyclone energy!'

Mia laughs. 'I'll try.'

They drive to the end of the track. She runs to the bus and climbs aboard.

'Hi, Shazza,' Mia says, wiping her feet carefully.

'G'day, Mia. How's the flooding at your place?'

'Not too bad, thanks.'

Mia sits in front of Jaxon, hoping he won't be annoying. He is, but she's able to mostly tune out his raucous laugh and stupid comments.

When Shazza pulls up at Wickham, Mia watches tourists paddling through the water to take selfies in front of the giant Haulpak. Their photos will have a true wet season feel.

Mia grips the seat as Kirra and Jess splash to the bus. They both have new blunt fringe haircuts. Like Erin's. Then she notices something worse. Her friends are not alone. Erin steps onto the bus with them.

'Hi, Mia,' Kirra calls. 'Look who's decided to go to school in Karratha for the next few months!'

Mia feels sick. Erin is wearing their daggy school uniform and somehow making it look fabulous.

'My dad's job is being extended,' Erin says, pushing past Mia to stop by Jaxon. 'Is this seat free?'

Jaxon gulps, looking like all his dreams have suddenly come true.

Mia chews a nail. This is really not what she needs today!

With both Erin and Jaxon sitting behind her, Mia squirms, feeling their eyes boring into the back of her head. When Kirra and Jess squeeze onto the seat beside her, she breathes a sigh of relief.

'Ready for your speech?' Jess asks.

'I think so.' Mia smiles. Last week her answer would have been a nervous 'no', but after the cyclone, the persuasive speech no longer seems like such a big deal. 'I read it to Nick during the cyclone. He reckons I should get a good mark . . .'

Jess raises her eyebrows.

'You know he's just a friend,' Mia tells her. 'We're both hatchling monitors. He understands the topic.'

She hears a laugh from the seat behind, then Kirra says, 'Good for you, Mia! If you get nervous, look our way.'

'Thanks, guys.'

'Now we'd better move before Shazza sees three of us sitting on one seat!'

Her friends shift to the opposite bench, but they lean across the aisle to chat.

'You should see the centre of town,' Jess tells her. 'Wickham looks like a war zone. The cyclone ripped up so many of the shade trees.'

'I loved those trees.' Mia does her best to sound casual, but she can't help staring at her friends' blunt fringes and touching her own wispy hair.

The highway is still flooded in some places. As Shazza eases their bus through the water, the little kids at the front wave to the emergency crews with their *Stop/Go* signs. Erin blabs on and on to Jaxon about some flooding at her house. *You're not the only one*, Mia thinks.

They pull up at school as the siren sounds.

'Want me to show you where the office is?' Jaxon offers.

'Thanks.' Erin beams. Mia notices her nails are not only intact, but freshly polished.

The bus door whooshes open, and Mia steps off with her friends.

'See you,' they call to Shazza.

She toots the horn in reply.

They race along the corridor to their English class.

'Those people who weren't able to present their speeches before the cyclone can do so today,' their teacher announces. 'Mia, you're first.'

'Go, Mia!' Kirra leans forward to listen.

'Thanks.' Mia hears the wobble in her voice and takes a deep breath. She walks to the front of the class and focuses on a point on the back wall. Then she grips her palm cards, remembering Bandit's terrified but trusting eyes as she removed the barbed wire.

'We were told to choose one issue,' Mia takes a deep breath, 'and I decided on climate change. When I began listing the urgent issues our generation faces, I felt overwhelmed, anxious, then sad . . . but sadness won't help our planet. We need to act.'

Mia's notes say *LOOK UP*, so she pauses, breathes deeply and makes brief eye contact with the back wall before continuing.

'Last December, at international climate talks, a Swedish girl accused world leaders of stealing her future. Those words have spread around the world. I believe we can all make a difference in our own way. Every action helps and carefully chosen words can change opinions.

'My speech is about marine protection, turtle conservation in particular, which is something I'm passionate about.

'Have you ever seen a turtle hatchling scampering down the beach? It's a beautiful sight. Some of you know that I volunteer at local beaches as a turtle hatchling monitor during the wet season, protecting nesting mothers and hatchlings.

'We also count turtle beach tracks and nests. This past wet season we recorded twenty-three nest sites at Boat Beach near Wickham but there could have been twice as many as that. Even though volunteers patrolled beaches for forty-one days, some nests were still disturbed by foxes, dogs, cats and off-road vehicles. It's estimated that only one turtle in every thousand makes it to adulthood.'

Mia blocks a sudden image of feral animals snatching hatchlings. She clutches her notes and continues.

'Humans pose the greatest threat to turtles, both in

the ocean and on land. Did you know that the temperature of sand on a nesting beach influences the sex of hatchlings?

'It's true. Warm sand creates more females, while cooler sand results in more male hatchlings. Global warming and rising sand temperatures are leading to the feminisation of some turtle species.'

A few of the boys hoot and whisper comments until Ms Malouf writes the word *Detention* on the board. She glares around the room, marker poised.

'And that's just one human-made problem.' Mia raises her voice. 'Plastic bags look like jellyfish and turtles love to eat jellyfish. But when they eat plastic their intestines become blocked. Then they starve to death. Microplastic kills many different kinds of marine creatures, including turtles.' Mia pauses. 'Some of these issues are hard to control. You can see why I felt so discouraged. What can *I* do to change all this?

'Luckily I'm not the only one who is worried. Lots of scientists, marine biologists and organisations are trying to help.

'Last year a turtle cooling project started on Milman Island, near the tip of Queensland. Volunteers built shade cloth structures to cool the sand, and regularly poured sea water over the nests.'

Mia glances at her friends. They both give a thumbs up.

'Trained volunteers are helping the turtles by moving eggs further away from the shoreline, and the Queensland Department of Environment and Heritage

Protection have shifted sand around the island to make a wider beach for the nesting turtles.

'Climate change impacts the habitats of so many creatures, not just turtles. We're the problem, but we can also be solutions. Each of us can be a citizen scientist.' Mia smiles as Jess pumps the air. 'I've joined an online group that reports strange wildlife sightings. It's fun and I'm becoming way more observant.

'Small choices made by many can have big effects. We can all do more.' Her voice becomes more purposeful. 'Ask your family not to drive on turtle beaches. Take your dogs to different beaches during nesting season, and don't let them roam the sand dunes. I've also learned that hatchlings are around seven times more likely to be eaten by predators on a beach with no jetty. Point Samson has a jetty but maybe we could ask the shire to build jetties near other nesting sites.'

Mia has practised the speech so many times that she barely needs her notes.

'There are so many things you can do. In the dry season we fundraise for turtle awareness programs. Buy our T-shirts, hats and keep cups to help our turtle program fund dune rehabilitation . . .'

The warning buzzer rings. As Mia reaches the end, she takes a moment to glance around. People still look interested!

'. . . And so, to conclude, like other marine creatures, turtles face increasing threats from both human behaviour and climate change. The problems can seem overwhelming. It's hard to not feel anxious, and want to give up, but let's do something instead. If we each choose a problem and take steps to improve things, we can all make a difference.

'I've made a list of environmental groups that need volunteers. Maybe you can sign up to help? I've chosen turtle protection and we need helpers at our Mother's Day stall . . .

'Thank you for listening.'

The buzzer rings. Her timing was perfect. As Mia gathers her palm cards, she takes a moment to enjoy her friends' cheers.

'Well done, Mia,' Ms Malouf says. 'You tackled both global and local problems and wove them together skilfully. I especially enjoyed the way you suggested positive solutions.'

As Mia sits down, Jess gives her a high five.

'That was great. Were you even nervous at all?'

Mia holds up her trembling hands.

Jess laughs. 'You hid it well! For a moment I thought my debating crown was threatened . . .'

'That crown is all yours. I'm just glad it's over!'

'Well, you nailed it,' Jess whispers as Ms Malouf checks her list.

Mia's skin tingles. Jess doesn't normally gush, so she knows her friend means it. Channelling her cyclone bravado worked! Good old Mum. Mia can't wait to text and tell her how well it went.

'Benjamin is next,' their teacher says. 'He's talking about sustainable burning practices.'

Now that her speech is over, Mia can relax. She leans back to listen to Ben.

'Traditional mosaic burning results in smaller fires and more sustainable outcomes. There are many ways this helps our environment. Slow burns give animals a chance to stay ahead of the flames, and fires can be lit when young animals, lizards and birds have grown and are able to get away . . .'

Ben's talk is interesting, but Mia's mind drifts. She's in the ocean swimming with hatchlings. Their little flippers are pumping through clear waves, with no predators in sight.

After Ben, Ruby suggests ways to tackle their feral cat problem. Other students speak about protecting mangroves, controlling cane toads, remote housing affordability, binge drinking and foetal alcohol syndrome. There are so many problems in their world. Mia feels her anxiety rise, then checks herself. Her peers are suggesting positive solutions. Then she sees people passing around her list of groups needing volunteers. It's full of names.

'We can be the change,' she whispers. 'We each have a voice, and I'm using mine to help my community.'

As the last speaker lists ways they can recycle, Mia sits straighter. These five-minute talks have sent out little ripples of change. It's a start . . .

Twenty-two

‖‖‖

Two weeks after the cyclone, Mia's backpack
is bulging with clothes to wear to the end-of-term movie
screening at the Karratha Red Earth Cinema. It's *Grease*
again, but Mia doesn't mind. She loves singing the old
songs. Kirra and Jess always sing along with her, but she
wonders whether they will today.

After the movie, the three of them are having a
sleepover in Kirra's shed. Jess invited Erin as well, and
Mia tried not to react when Jess told them the older girl
couldn't make it.

'Everything ready?' Mum asks as she clears the
breakfast bowls.

Mia double-checks her sleepover backpack: pyjamas,
toilet bag and plenty of snacks. Then she wheels her
suitcase into the hallway. Mum's driving her to Karratha
after equine therapy tomorrow to catch the flight to
Perth. Mia has face paint and brushes for the twins'
birthday party on Sunday.

'All packed,' she tells Mum. 'I just need to add my toilet bag tomorrow.'

They drive to the bus stop and Shazza pulls up beside the van.

'Enjoy the movie and sleepover,' Mum says. 'I'll see you before the first riders arrive tomorrow.'

'Okay.'

Shazza is wearing her wildest 'last day of term' caftan and rainbow hairclips. With Jaxon too busy gazing at Erin to bother her, Mia enjoys the bus ride to Karratha.

'I've put swags on the floor,' Kirra tells them along the way. 'Dad's stacked the fire pit and I have a bag of marshmallows ready to roast.'

Jess looks out at the sky and says, 'If the clouds clear, we might see the space station while they're roasting.'

Nothing much happens at school on the last day of term. Their teachers hand back tests and assignments and Mia is excited to receive a credit for her persuasive talk.

'Soon we'll be doing TEDx talks together,' Jess jokes.

'That's not likely!'

The movie is great. They sing all the old songs and then do a few moves as Kirra's dad drives them home from the cinema. Their friendship triangle feels balanced and whole. Mia watches pastel colours smudge the clouds. She loves the wide Pilbara sky, especially at dusk when soft light glows on the pale tree trunks and corellas argue over roosting sites.

'The sky is like a huge science experiment,' Jess says,

then she explains about light waves scattering as they meet the atmosphere until they all tell her to stop.

Kirra's mum makes the best sausage rolls in Wickham and their shed picnic is a feast. There's pizza, popcorn and fruit sticks. After dinner they change into pyjamas and Kirra brings out old photo albums. The girls sit around the fire pit, licking melted marshmallows off sticks and laughing at the faded images.

'You guys were cute,' Jess tells them as stars appear in the sky.

'Hey, remember when the *Red Dog* film came out?' Kirra says. 'And that game we made up.'

'Being Red Dog?' Mia asks.

'Yes! And you used to wander around the garden, pretending to pee on all the trees.'

'What?' Jess interrupts. 'I've never heard this story.'

Kirra cracks up. 'When we were little, each tree in the garden was meant to be a different town that Red Dog visited!'

Jess points to a tall palm. 'What was that one?'

Mia and Kirra both shout, 'Roebourne.'

'And that one?'

'Dampier.'

They burst into laughter again.

Kirra's dad comes out. 'Sorry to interrupt the fun, but how about an early swim tomorrow before I drop Mia home?'

'Yes!'

'I'll wake you at seven.'

They lie side by side in their swags, staring at the

stars. Jess points to the space station and they track its orbit. As Mia falls asleep to the buzzing of locust wings, she knows there'll be no bad dreams tonight.

In the morning they eat an early breakfast, then grab beach towels.

'Only half an hour of swimming,' Kirra's dad tells them. 'I promised Zara I'd get Mia home before the horse sessions begin.'

They race across the sand and see Nick spearfishing near the rocks. He lifts his mask, waves and swims to shore.

'I'd better put aside the spear gun while you're swimming.' He laughs, making a shark fin sign.

'Is that your boat?' Jess points to a tinny on the sand.

'Technically it's Dad's runabout, but I'm using it while he's in Perth.'

'When does he get back?' Mia asks.

'Tomorrow, with Mum and Lexi.' Nick nods to the spear gun. 'I'm hoping to make fresh seafood chowder.'

'Yum. Say hi to them from me.'

'Okay. Lexi's not happy. She loves her Perth school. If your mum has a lesson available, some horse-time might sweeten the coming-home deal.'

'I'm pretty sure there's a place,' Mia tells him. She isn't expecting Erin to return. 'I'll check which time with Mum.'

'That'd be great.'

'Bandit will be excited to see Lexi.'

Jess points to the runabout and asks, 'So, when are you going to take Mia and her friends out to the island for a snorkel?'

Nick laughs. 'How about next month when everything settles down and there's no chance of another cyclone?'

'Okay,' Jess crosses her arms, 'we won't let you forget.'

Mia shakes her head, embarrassed, but Nick smiles. 'I won't.'

'Race you in,' Kirra yells.

They sprint to the shoreline, dive through the waves and swim out deeper.

As they tread water, Mia smiles at her friends and begins doing cephalopod arms. Oops. She stops, remembering Kirra's reaction last time.

There's an awkward pause, then Kirra raises her strong arms and wraps Mia in a massive cephalopod hug. They tumble under the waves while Jess laughs.

'You guys are impossible,' she says, then joins the huddle.

Twenty-three

‖‖‖

'I'm back! How cool was the cyclone?' Rosa signs. 'Were you scared?'

Mia nods and spells out *Terrified!* She hesitates, wanting to ask Rosa how the wind *felt* for her, but unsure whether that would be intrusive.

'What?' Rosa signs.

'For me, the sound of the wind was the scariest thing, but what was it like for you?'

'I felt wind whipping against my skin and saw trees bending,' Rosa grins and points to her cowboy boots, 'and a rumbling feeling came through the ground into my feet!'

They ride around the circuit, splashing through shrinking puddles, then stop to watch a flock of zebra finches. Rosa looks happy as she signs, 'Too wet today for creepy bungarra lizard.'

Mia laughs. 'I still like them,' she replies, looking around to see whether she can spot the goanna.

After wheedling an extra ten minutes, Rosa trots

Sultan into the home yard for his rub-down. Sultan nuzzles his little friend until she giggles, making Mia laugh too as she prepares Freckles for the next rider.

Rosa suddenly taps her boots. She points across the yard and signs, 'Wow.'

Erin is striding across the muddy yard in a flash new pair of R.M. Williams boots. Mia groans.

'Nice boots,' she mutters as Erin comes closer. 'I didn't expect to see you this morning.' Mia bites her lip, wondering whether her words sounded nasty.

'Thanks, I ordered them online. They're more practical than those other ones.'

Rosa's dad arrives to collect Rosa. The girl hugs Sultan, waves to Mia and signs, 'See ya.'

'Bye, Rosa.'

There's an awkward silence before Erin asks, 'How did your sandbagging hold up?'

'All good.' Mia decides not to tell Erin about the other dramas. The less she shares with her the better. 'How about yours?'

'Surprisingly well.'

After another silence, Mia says, 'Well, you survived your first cyclone. I guess you're a Pilbara girl now.'

'What an initiation! The wind was like a jet engine and that torrential rain went on forever. Our front room was flooded.'

'Most cyclones don't hang around that long,' Mia tells her. 'Veronica was strange.'

Erin looks around. 'Where's Bandit?'

'Still recovering. We set the horses free during the worst of it, that's the safest thing to do, but Bandit got tangled in some wire.'

'Oh no.'

'We aren't sure where it happened. All I know is that he came home with deep cuts.'

'Poor fellow.'

'He needed five stitches.' Mia calls Bandit and he hobbles across the yard. Mia strokes his muzzle and points to the row of neat stitches, feeling rather proud of her work.

'But I heard your mum was stuck out at a cattle station during the cyclone?' Erin looks confused.

'She was.'

'So who did the stitches?' Erin's jaw drops open as she realises. 'Did *you* sew him up?'

Mia nods, trying not to look smug as she watches Erin's disbelief.

After another awkward pause, Mia says, 'It was touch and go for a while. Bandit's healing well, but he's not strong enough yet for riding.'

'Okay.' Erin still looks surprised.

'But you can feed and pet him.'

'Okay,' she repeats.

'Did you want a session today?' Mia asks, trying not to look confused.

'I organised it with your mum last night.'

'She must have forgotten to tell me.'

'Is that okay?'

'Of course.'

They glance over at Sultan.

'He's really gentle . . .' Mia tells her.

Erin takes a deep breath. 'All right,' she says. 'If you lead me, I'll give it a go.'

'Sure.'

Mia strides over to the tall racehorse before Erin has a chance to change her mind. She leads Sultan to the mounting tower and waits while Erin clambers into the saddle.

'Ready?'

Erin nods, so Mia clicks her tongue. 'Walk on,' she tells Sultan.

As they circle the home paddock, Mia feels her shoulders relax. She no longer needs Erin to like or even accept her. Veronica left her a gift of confidence, or at least *a little bit more* confidence than before.

Not caring about the older girl's opinion feels like shrugging off a heavy cloak. Mia looks down at her sturdy boots and horsey-smelling jeans. They're her second skin and they do just fine.

Erin's posture sways in time with Sultan's steady gait. Silence settles between them and Mia knows that whatever happens, she wants to become a vet and continue Mum's work in equine therapy. It's what she was born to do. There'll be other cyclones along the way to challenge her, but hopefully none as slow moving as Veronica.

'Are you going to the beach today?' Erin asks, jolting Mia's thoughts back to the present.

Mia shakes her head. 'After the sessions, Mum's

driving me to Karratha. I'm catching the afternoon flight to Perth to stay with my dad.'

'Lucky!'

'Hmm, maybe not. I'm helping to organise a party for my two-year-old siblings tomorrow.'

'Good luck with that.' Erin laughs. The new girl looks down at her beautiful boots for a moment then adds, 'I'm sorry if I sounded mean at Wickham, and on the bus . . . When I'm nervous, I say stupid things.'

Now it's Mia's jaw that drops open in surprise. *Could someone as stylish and self-assured as Erin really get nervous?* For a moment Mia's too gobsmacked to reply, then she says, 'Me too!'

They laugh and the awkwardness between them lifts a little.

'The way everyone helped us after the cyclone made me see the community differently.'

Mia nods. 'I like the way people here look out for each other.' She pauses, then asks, 'Do you like riding Sultan?'

'When I don't look down I do, and you know, from this height, the red earth and spinifex do have a special kind of beauty . . .'

Mia grins.

'You never know, I might even grow to like it here!'

They chat about the cyclone, school and other kids on the bus. The forty-minute session races past and Mia is surprised when it's time to stop.

'Thanks,' Erin says as Mia leads the big horse to the mounting tower. She dismounts and hesitates for a moment, scuffing her new boots in the dirt, then asks, 'What do you know about Jaxon?'

Mia is gobsmacked all over again. She tries to think of something positive about hyenas.

'Umm, I know that he really likes you.'

'Do you think so?' Erin blushes, looking pleased, and Mia grins, incapable of hiding her shock. Firstly, that Erin hasn't noticed that he likes her, and second, Jaxon? *Really?* Of all the guys at school . . .

'Yep, he sure does.'

'He has a cute smile, doesn't he?'

Mia thinks for a moment. *Has he?* In all those years of Jaxon mocking her on the bus, she's somehow missed noticing his smile. Mia gives Jaxon's smile the benefit of the doubt and nods.

'I reckon Sultan's ready for a treat,' she says, changing the subject.

Erin holds her hand flat to feed him a carrot. Sultan takes it gently, then rubs his furry head against her jeans.

'He likes you.'

'I like him too, and he didn't dribble on my shirt.'

When all the clients have left, Mia checks that the sweaty horses have been thoroughly rubbed down. She fills their feed troughs, then runs back to the house to change into clean jeans and a fresh shirt.

'Everything packed?' Mum asks.

'Yep.' Mia wheels her case to the van, then whistles to Biff. She opens the door and the kelpie jumps onto the back seat. 'Let's go.'

Mum hands Mia a parcel. 'Can you squeeze this into your backpack?'

'Sure, what is it?'

'A present for Timmy and Tilda. I'm hoping it'll help soften your dad's opinion of me.'

'It wasn't your fault,' Mia replies, pushing the parcel into her bag. 'I was the one who kept telling you I was okay and to go to Spinifex Downs.'

'I know,' Mum says with a sigh, 'but I'm meant to be the adult who protects you.'

'If you'd been here protecting me, I wouldn't have had my first patient.'

'That's true! And you did an amazing job. I'm so proud of you.'

'I hope Dad will be too, once I explain it all again.'

'He will.'

At the airport, Mia checks her case in, then they sit at the café, waiting for departure.

'I'm glad everything worked out with Raven and little Arrow.'

'So am I,' Mum replies, 'and with Lorenzo and Bandit. What a team!'

Mia's phone pings with a message from Dad.

See you at the airport!

As if on cue her departure is announced.

The flight to Perth is now boarding through Gate One.

Mia texts Dad.

Flight is on time.

She can't wait to see him. Phone-planning the party with Elena has brought her closer to her stepmum, but time alone with Dad will always be special. She has photos of Bandit's stitches ready to show him, and Dad said they all want to hear her speech, so she's packed the palm cards as well. Maybe they'll stop at their favourite café on the way home to share a banana milkshake . . .

'Time to go,' Mum says.

Mia gives her mother an enormous hug, then walks onto the steamy tarmac with the other passengers.

As the plane leaves the runway, angling steeply into a lapis lazuli sky, Mia looks down at the rugged Pilbara landscape. Patterns of ancient waterways snake across the red-brown country, like the branching roots of enormous trees. Veronica's floodwater glistens in a few areas, but most has now soaked into the earth.

Mia touches her blue necklace and thinks about all the things that have happened over the past few weeks. Some good, some terrifying, but Veronica has left her with a better sense of who she is and what she wants to become.

Mia gazes out the window as the airbus settles into a cruising altitude. The sky ahead is clear and there's no turbulence. She has plenty of new turtle volunteers and people in her class have signed up to help other organisations. Taking action has helped overcome her anxiety. With support from her family and friends, there's nothing she can't do.

Author's Note

|||||||||||||||||||||||||||||||||||||||||||||||||||||||||||||||||||||||||||||

The Pilbara region of Western Australia is a place of great natural beauty, with dramatic rocks, sparkling oceans, red pindan soil and spinifex. The sky feels impossibly wide, especially with the pastel colours of sunset when raucous parrots swirl down to settle on trees. This region is also a place of harsh contrasts: extreme heat, cyclonic winds and torrential rain. I have tried to capture these rich, sensory impressions in my writing.

Mia's story takes place on the lands of the Ngarluma, Yindjibarndi and Banyjima people. European settlement and the impacts of pastoral and mining industries have resulted in terrible suffering for First Nations people of the Pilbara. While this book does not explore those injustices, as an author I needed to fully understand my setting. Researching the social history of this area was confronting. Early settlers brought smallpox and influenza leading to countless deaths; massacres occurred, including the infamous Flying Foam Massacre of 1868. Indigenous people were kidnapped to work in the pearling industry; entire communities were forced to relocate onto other lands. Children were stolen. Sacred sites were polluted.[1]

The demands of the pastoral and mining industries also hugely affected the natural landscape and environment. Introduced animals began competing with native species on fragile land. Now, feral cats, goats, foxes, camels, donkeys, pigs, horses and wild dogs cause widespread damage to waterways and native vegetation, leading to soil erosion as well as predation of native animals.

Massive mining infrastructure overshadows ports and towns, with rail networks snaking inland to enormous open-cut mines. Traditional custodians' use of mosaic fire-burning practices, used for thousands of years to care for country, has been interrupted.[2]

The Pilbara is the powerhouse of the Australian economy, providing a substantial chunk of Australia's annual GDP (Gross Domestic Product). Every day huge trainloads of iron ore are extracted from mines across the region and transported to ports to be shipped around the world. In 2019, mining company Rio Tinto launched the world's first automated heavy-haul rail network. This driverless system can move around one million tonnes of iron ore a day.

---

1 https://apo.org.au/sites/default/files/resource-files/2002-12/apo-nid94521.pdf

2 https://www.dfes.wa.gov.au/site/documents/Cultural-and-Contemporary-Fire-Practices.pdf

Development has come at great cost. Despite environmental guidelines, while I was writing this story, the Juukan Gorge rock shelters, sacred sites cared for by the Puutu Kunti Kurrama and Pinikura (Binigura) peoples for tens of thousands of years, were destroyed by Rio Tinto.[3]

Rock art of the Burrup Peninsula and Dampier Archipelago dates back about 40000 years. There are hundreds of thousands of images in an area near Dampier Port, close to two large fertiliser plants.[4] At the time of writing, the area remains unprotected.[5]

Mia's story is mostly set between the towns of Wickham and Point Samson. In 1902–03, a deep-water jetty was built at Point Samson to service towns in the region. The original T-head jetty, nearly 600 metres long, was destroyed by a cyclone in 1925. The remaining part of the jetty was damaged by Cyclone Orson in 1989. Point Samson is now home to around 300 people,

---

3 https://www.aboriginalheritagecouncil.vic.gov.
   au/1-year-destruction-juukan-gorge-and-nothing-has-changed
   https://www.riotinto.com/news/inquiry-into-juukan-gorge
   https://www.mediastatements.wa.gov.au/Pages/McGowan/2021/10/
   McGowan-Government-welcomes-Senate-Inquiry-Final-Report-
   into-Juukan-Gorge.aspx

4 https://www.sbs.com.au/nitv/nitv-news/article/2018/03/23/worlds-
   largest-rock-art-collection-could-be-destroyed-within-century
   https://www.fara.com.au/wp-content/uploads/2018/01/Evidence-
   of-destruction-of-rock-patina-on-Burrup-Peninsula-May17.pdf

5 https://www.theguardian.com/australia-news/2022/mar/12/
   fertiliser-company-urged-to-halt-plans-to-remove-burrup--
   peninsula-indigenous-rock-art

and bloated cattle really did wash up on the beach after Cyclone Veronica.

Wickham was developed as a mining company town in 1972 to support operations at the Cape Lambert port facility. The population is around 3000, most of whom work in the iron-ore industry.

Much of the land between Point Samson and Wickham is Crown land or used for mining. I spent many hours exploring the region trying to settle on a place for Mia's home. Pilbara Animal Care is fictitious, and in my imagination, the property is off a track, a little north of town. Spinifex Downs is also a fictitious location, situated in the general area between Mundabullangana and Whim Creek.

My home is 3000 kilometres from the setting of Mia's story, in Albany/Kinjarling on the south coast, home of Menang Noongar people. While I have not experienced the terror of a cyclone, during a ferocious storm in Albany, with winds of around one hundred and twenty kilometres per hour, the balcony of my lounge room crashed away. I was so grateful for the help of volunteer State Emergency Services.

I regularly visit the Pilbara to speak at schools and libraries, and was very happy to return to research this book. The story takes place near the resting site of Red Dog, the Pilbara wanderer. His story featured in a book by Louis de Bernières that was subsequently made into a movie which has become an Australian classic. I also loved visiting Cossack, the old pearling ghost town originally known as Tien Tsin. It's one of my favourite places in the Pilbara.

Hatchling Cove was inspired by visits to beaches near Port Walcott Yacht Club, including Boat Beach and nearby turtle nesting areas. Each year turtles arrive to lay their eggs; however, the effects of climate change now challenge their survival. Warming water currents and beaches degraded by storms of increasing ferocity can interrupt breeding cycles. Fortunately, there are many organisations and hatchling monitors doing all they can to help.

I am grateful for the hospitality and assistance of people living in 'Cyclone Alley'; Karratha, Port Hedland, Wickham and Point Samson. Their names are listed in the acknowledgements and their support helped bring Cyclone Veronica to life in my imagination.

Acknowledgements

This story was written mostly on Menang Noongar country in the south-west. My research also took me to areas around Karratha, Roebourne, Wickham and Point Samson – the lands of the Ngarluma, Yindjibarndi and Banyjima people. I would like to acknowledge the traditional owners of the land where this story was written and takes place.

Many people have helped bring *Mia* to life. Thanks to Helena Mead, Sally Culver and the wonderful team at Karratha Library for sharing cyclone details and organising the workshop that led me to Kelly Nunn and her daughter Tahlia from Wickham, who then introduced me to Kirsten Bouzaid in Point Samson.

Huge thanks to Bruce Jorgensen, CEO of the Ngarluma Yindjibarndi Foundation and his wife, Cath, for inviting travellers into their home, introducing us to their friends, explaining local history and showing us more of the wonders of the Cossack and Point Samson regions.

At the City of Karratha offices, thank you to Susan Babao and Laurinda Timmins for showing me land management maps and talking through horseriding possibilities. In Port Hedland, thank you to the terrific library team, especially Gill Westera and Lisa Taylor, for sharing your experiences and images taken during Cyclone Veronica.

I'm indebted to Karratha mobile vet, Dr Lisa Pearce, for advice regarding horses and Pilbara wildlife. Not only did Lisa teach me about animal care before, during and after a cyclone, she also took me to her remote bush hideaway to introduce me to her own beautiful horses. Lisa's practical energy and kindness infuses every horse scene. Enormous thanks also to Drisana Levitzke-Gray, Young Australian of the Year 2015, Brent Levitzke and Kristen Levitzke for advice regarding Deaf community references, as well as my friend Lucy Stuart for introducing us.

Thank you, Helen Burnett, for medical advice, and Maree Dawes for insightful and sensitive discussion regarding panic attacks and anxiety. High country hugs to Karen Davidson and Owen Davis for sharing your off-grid living experiences, explaining the intricacies of generators and for being a sounding board on contentious brumby issues.

Huge bouquets to my skilled draft readers, Sophie Wolfer and Deb Fitzpatrick, for going over and above. Thanks also to Peter Watson, Audrey Davidson, Karen and Owen, Kate Woodward, Frané Lessac, Sian Turner, Emma Crook, Beth Kirkland, Barbara Temperton and Kavisha Roberts for editing advice.

As always, thank you to my agent, Clive Newman, for managing the practical things. Enormous thanks to the wonderful team at Allen & Unwin, especially Lyn White and Hilary Reynolds for wise and insightful editing. It's an honour to be part of this important, award-winning series which helps younger readers navigate climate change across Australia.

Being an active member of the Australian writing community is important to me. I support local chapters of SCBWI and Story Dogs and am a Room to Read ambassador. I am deeply grateful for financial support from the Western Australian Department of Local Government, Sport and Cultural Industries, which allowed me valued writing time to complete a first draft of this story.

Timeline

2019 18 March

A tropical low-pressure system forms about 550 km north of Broome in Western Australia.

20 March 3 a.m. (AWST) Australian Western Standard Time

The system intensifies and is currently north-west of Broome. The Australian Bureau of Meteorology (BOM) upgrades the slow-moving system to a Category 1 tropical cyclone, naming it 'Veronica'.

Over the next 12 hours Veronica is reclassified as a Category 2, then a Category 3 cyclone with core winds estimated to be up to 220 km per hour. A long period of damaging winds is forecast to impact communities from Port Hedland to Karratha.

The Pilbara coast braces for widespread destruction, storm surges, strong winds and flooding. A Blue Alert is issued for coastal communities including Karratha and Port Hedland. Residents are advised to reinforce their homes with sandbags and stock up on food and water supplies.

21 March

Cyclone Veronica is reclassified as a Category 4 cyclone as it travels south towards the Pilbara coast before attaining Category 5 status with extreme wind gusts.

A prolonged period of gale and storm force winds estimated at 195 km per hour and heavy rainfall lash Port Hedland, Karratha and other smaller communities that remain on Blue Alert. Peak wind gusts of 275 km per hour are recorded in some areas.

Tides peak well above the normal high-tide mark due to significant storm surges. Widespread flooding occurs, causing evacuations in the Port Hedland area.

22 March

Cyclone Veronica is downgraded to Category 4 as it nears the coast. Authorities warn the slow-moving system poses the biggest risk to the region in a decade, as it will persist for longer than a typical cyclone.

Cyclone Veronica is expected to make landfall on Sunday morning. Alerts are in place for Pardoo and Mardie. Pilbara coast residents are told to activate emergency cyclone plans.

The port of Port Hedland – the most valuable export hub in Australia and one of the largest iron ore–loading ports in the world – is closed. Evacuation centres are set up in Karratha and Port Hedland. Mine workers are sent home and iron-ore ships head out to sea. Rio Tinto's Cape Lambert and Dampier ports are cleared as a precautionary measure. A Yellow Alert is issued for residents between Pardoo and Mardie, including Port Hedland, South Hedland, Point Samson, Wickham, Roebourne, Karratha, Barrow Island and Dampier.

Pilbara coastal communities are warned to expect deteriorating conditions with more destructive winds, hazardous storm surges and heavy rainfall causing major flooding. A severe flood watch is forecast for much of the Pilbara, with some areas set to receive between 100 and 500 mm of rain, more than their annual rainfall in just a few days.

A Red Alert is issued for the Hedland region. Heavy rainfall is forecast to cut roads and isolate communities. More than 179 mm of rain has been recorded in Port Hedland in the past 24 hours, with powerful winds tearing through the town.

23 March

Prolonged heavy rainfall leads to flooding and is expected to continue throughout the day. The coastal community of Roebourne records wind gusts up to 154 km per hour. The Department of Fire and Emergency Services (DFES) predicts significant storm surges for parts of the Pilbara coast, with a high risk of inundation to properties in Port Hedland.

Cyclone Veronica approaches the coast. High tides force water onshore. Rainfall in excess of 500 mm is predicted, cutting roads and further isolating communities.

24 March

Cyclone Veronica stalls 80 km off the Pilbara coast, gradually weakening. The eye of the cyclone finally reaches land about halfway between Karratha and Port Hedland just to the north of Wickham about 40 km off the coast, and is expected to remain near the coast on Sunday night.

The BOM reports tide levels of 1.5 m above normal levels at Port Hedland. A Red Alert is issued for Pardoo to Mardie. Residents urged to take shelter immediately.

Hundreds of homes across the Pilbara are without power and State Emergency Services (SES) workers are unable to offer assistance due to heavy rain and extreme wind gusts. Residents are advised to avoid waterways till flooding eases.

The cyclone pummels the coast for 24 hours, bringing down powerlines and damaging buildings. Wind gusts up to 220 km per hour are recorded east of Roebourne.

25 March

Cyclone Veronica begins to weaken more quickly as it moves in a westerly direction parallel to the coast. Conditions in Port Hedland ease, but flooding remains the main concern for authorities and residents. Schools remain closed. Residents begin the recovery process while rain continues to fall in many areas. Alerts at Port Hedland are lifted and emergency crews begin to assess damages and restore power.

26 March – 27 March

Cyclone Veronica continues westward and is finally downgraded to a tropical low to the west of Karratha, passing Exmouth on 27 March. Rainfall totals along the Pilbara coast and adjacent inland areas between Port Hedland and Karratha were 5 to 7 times the March average.

Cyclone Veronica's intensity lessens and, after making landfall on North West Cape later that day, it begins to track away from the Australian mainland. Due to the community's preparedness for the cyclone, no deaths or significant injuries have been reported.

Port Hedland has been impacted by major flooding and roofs from homes thrown across the area, causing up to $45 million in damage. Thousands of people are affected with businesses forced to evacuate.

Residents begin dealing with the aftermath as pastoralists conduct aerial surveys to locate missing cattle. About 2000 cattle are dead, many washed up on local beaches.

Most of the Pilbara's coastal regions have suffered some level of damage.

Economic losses primarily from disrupted iron-ore exports total about $1.7 billion, making Cyclone Veronica one of West Australia's costliest weather events. BHP's iron-ore production is reduced by an estimated 6–8 million tonnes, Rio Tinto's by approximately 14 million tonnes, and Fortescue Metals' production by an estimated 2 million tonnes.

The port of Port Hedland reopens. Commonwealth–State Disaster Recovery Funding Arrangements claims for Cyclone Veronica total about $36.7 million. Most of the claims are from the Town of Port Hedland and City of Karratha for the restoration of public assets.

Find out more about . . .

Cyclone Veronica
https://www.abc.net.au/news
Search for 'Cyclone Veronica rapidly intensifies off
WA's Pilbara coast'

https://www.abc.net.au/btn
Search for 'Cyclones Explained'

http://www.bom.gov.au/cyclone/history/veronica.shtml

www.youtube.com
Search for 'Severe Weather Update: severe tropical
cyclone Veronica, Sunday 24 March 2019'
Search for 'Understanding tropical cyclone categories'

https://climatecouncil.org.au
Search for 'Cyclone Factsheet'

Pilbara, Western Australia
https://kids.kiddle.co/Pilbara

https://www.australiasnorthwest.com/explore/pilbara

https://www.bbc.com/travel/article/20220126-is-the-
pilbara-the-oldest-place-on-earth

Climate Change and the Pilbara
https://www.agric.wa.gov.au/climate-change/
climate-pilbara-region-western-australia

Turtle Conservation
www.youtube.com
Search for 'West Pilbara Turtle Program volunteers'
West Pilbara Turtle Program
WIRES Turtle Conservation
Australian Marine Conservation Society
Care for Hedland Turtle Monitoring
WWF Adopt a Sea Turtle

Protecting Marine Life
https://www.marineconservation.org.au

Caring for Pilbara Wildlife
https://pwca.org.au/

Citizen Scientist
https://www.redmap.org.au/region/wa/

Climate Anxiety
https://www.kidshelpline.com.au

https://ww.headspace.com

See Teachers' Notes for helpful references

Red Dog
https://www.reddogwa.com/where_was_red_dog_buried

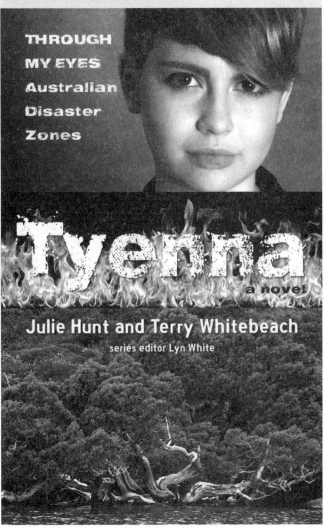

THROUGH
MY EYES
Australian
Disaster
Zones

Tyenna
a novel

Julie Hunt and Terry Whitebeach
series editor Lyn White

An engaging and suspenseful novel about one girl's experience of the terrifying Tasmanian bushfires.

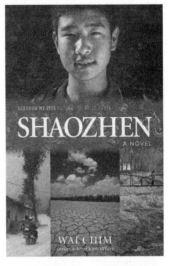

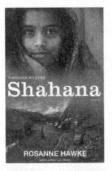
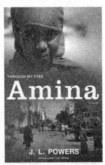
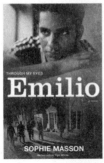

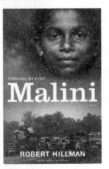